CALLS FROM THE GRANITE STATE

Calls *from the* Granite State

stories by

RICHARD MERRILL

JOHN DANIEL & COMPANY

SANTA BARBARA · 1997

Printed in the United States of America

The following stories, some in slightly different form, have previously appeared in *Antaeus:* "The Disappearance," "In El's Feeling Sorry for My Mother's Old Boyfriends," "Fancy Cars and Their Owners," "The Recovery," and "The Billboard."

Published by John Daniel & Company
A division of Daniel and Daniel, Publishers, Inc.
Post Office Box 21922
Santa Barbara, CA 93121

Book design: Eric Larson

LIBRARY OF CONGRESS CATALOGING-IN-PUBLICATION DATA
Merrill, Richard 1956–1994.
Calls from the Granite State : stories / Richard Merrill.
p. cm.
ISBN 1-880284-22-7 (cloth : alk. paper)
1. New Hampshire—Social life and customs—Fiction. 2. Working class—New Hampshire—Fiction. I. Title
PS3563.E74525C35 1997
813.54—DC20 96-42280
CIP

To those who were bound to Rich
by bonds of love.

The family and friends of Richard Merrill
are indebted to John L'Heureux,
author, teacher, friend,
who agreed to edit this posthumous collection of stories.
He is the editor Rich himself would have chosen.

Contents

Preface

I met Richard Merrill in October, 1979, when he was the youngest and I, more than thirty years older, was one of the oldest of the ten participants in that year's Stanford Writing Program. By then, two of his stories had appeared in the very prestigious *Antaeus.* At first I was mostly impressed by his early success, but as the weeks went by, and we read and criticized each other's stories, his modesty, his kindness, and his sensitivity became apparent, and my admiration developed into affection.

He wrote of those whom we call, for want of a better term, "little people." In one of our sessions someone—indeed someone who himself had never had anything published—condemned these people as "worthless," indeed as "animals," not worth reading or writing about. It was of course an outrageous remark, but the convention in the workshop was to listen to each other's comments, to accept or reject them, but not to try to defend one's work. Rich listened in silence, nodding, giving no intimation of hurt or resentment. He didn't abandon his subject, however, and it was precisely his sympathy for, and his devotion to, his "little people" that—at the time—I respected most in his work.

When our year in the program ended, he left Palo Alto, and I lost touch with him, and it was not until eight years later when he phoned to congratulate me on the publication of my own first book, that our friendship resumed. I saw him last in Los Angeles in the spring of 1991, when we spent a wonderful day together, and, though we remained in touch with each other, I saw nothing of what he had later written till after his death.

Only then, when I saw the full body of his work, did I see the rest of what Rich had been saying. He had been writing about an environment, and about a person born in it, no longer fully at home in it, but forever bound to it by sympathy, loyalty, and profound affection. He wrote of entrapment—of the need to break away from what prevents one from becoming what one needs to be, and of the difficulty of achieving freedom. And he wrote about a sense of obligation, of responsibility—not only to individuals and family, but to the wider community and even to the outcast.

His life and work were much too soon cut short.

MAE BRISKIN

EDITOR'S NOTE

Rich Merrill was a student of mine, and a friend, and a fine, accomplished writer. When Mae Briskin and Jack Corwin suggested that I edit this collection of stories by Rich, I was happy to do so.

To say, however, that I have edited these stories is to suggest that I may have altered them. I have not. His stories are presented here exactly as Rich presented them to magazine editors when he first wrote them.

I have done this: I have put them in their present order, made the few minimal changes that Rich himself would have made (caught and corrected accidental misspellings, variations in punctuation, the odd unnecessary repetition of words), and throughout this process I have made it my guiding principle to preserve and present his voice and vision.

Rich Merrill's voice was rare, deceptively simple and straightforward, with a generous undertone of sympathy and understanding. His vision was unique, uplifting, deeply humane.

I am pleased to have had a small part in preserving and presenting that voice and vision.

JOHN L'HEUREUX

CALLS FROM THE GRANITE STATE

The Smart One in the Family

AS THE BUS SWINGS out from under Manhattan and churns up the Jersey Pike, he can't believe where he's headed. Not west, to California, as planned, but north, to his parents' in New Hampshire!

He can't believe where he's headed, and he can't imagine what he's going to find.

"You know, Tom," his mother said on the phone four nights ago, "you have always been the one things happen to."

"I've always been the one things happen to?"

"That's right, Tom," she said, "you have. In school. At work. Think about it. People have always recognized your talents. More importantly, they've rewarded you for them. Bud hasn't had much of that."

"They've rewarded me? *Who's* rewarded me?"

"Is it really necessary to repeat everything I say?"

"You mean I wish they rewarded me."

"No. I mean…oh, Tom, you know what I mean. So just cut it out, please."

In school? He'd been no great shake. *At work? What* work? The firm he'd given his guts to had canned him after all. Had she forgotten that already?

No, he didn't know what she meant, not really; but it was late, so he let it drop. He switched the receiver from one ear to the other. "Anyway," he said, knowing he was asking for an earful, "just tell me how it happened."

His mother had phoned to tell him that Bud, his brother, had finally spent a night in jail. Bud, who was a year and a half older than Tom (and who had left his job at the gypsum plant three years ago to play in a rock group that, like all the others since, broke up a few months later), still lived at home.

"Well," his mother started, "this new band that your brother is in, they were practicing out at the Millers'."

But before she got any further she said, "They're not bad, Tom, by the way. They're a lot better than any of the others have been. Bud had me listen to a tape they made and...."

"*Please*, Mother. It's late."

So she started in again. She told him that while his brother's new band was practicing out at the Millers', evidently one of the Millers' neighbors complained and the police came and made them stop. That was when they decided to load up the equipment, she said, and move the rehearsal, kit and caboodle, to Owen's.

"*Owen's?*" Tom said. "Who's Owen?"

"Owen I-don't-know-his-last-name. All I know is that he lives in a trailer out at the end of Spinney Road. On a lot right next to the Edgewood Manor Nursing Home, I'm afraid, and just a skip from the A.S.P.C.A."

She told him that by the time they got there and got their equipment set up, it was two-thirty when they plugged in their amps. And then, when they started to *play*.... "*Well*," she said, "you can just picture it, I'm sure. This Owen's trailer nearly shook off its blocks. And the dogs at the A.S.P.C.A., every single one of them started to howl."

"Okay, okay," Tom said.

"You asked me how it happened. 'Disturbing the peace' was the less serious charge. The more serious...well, it was the same officers who'd shown up at the Millers' apparently, and when the younger one banged on the door they slammed it in his face."

"*Okay*," Tom said again. And then she told him about the fine.

"Four-hundred-and-eighty-six dollars," she said. "That's a little steep, Tom, I think, don't you? Considering it was only half that when they stopped him for driving after his license had expired. And when he left the empty six-pack on the picnic table at Prescott Park...that was how much? Fifty-eight? Seems like a bargain now," she mused. "I never could understand how people could litter. *That,* Tom, seems to me to be a whole lot worse than waking up a handful of old people. And it couldn't have been more than that!" she added quickly. "Not at that hour. With all of their hearing aids turned off."

When Tom pointed out that she was making excuses for him again, her first reaction was "No, I'm not, Tom. Am I?" But then, when she'd thought about it, she said, "Well, Tom, maybe you're right."

"Of course I'm right!" he said.

"I had to go to the bank and cash a CD," she continued. "Four-hundred-and-eighty-six dollars! But, Tom, please," she said. "It's not the money. What's money? It's that the police sergeant in charge was my cousin Ruth's first husband. Tom, I do have *some* pride left, you know. And your brother, he is twenty-eight."

"Yes, Mother. I know."

"*And your father...*"

Oh, Christ, here it comes, Tom thought.

"Your father has been no help at all. All he does is sit in front of that damn idiot box. But, I suppose I shouldn't be surprised. He's never been able to deal with these things. And I don't mean just recently either. Remember when your uncle left Aunt Molly? Remember when you were a baby and you nearly died of colic? Well, no, I guess you wouldn't, not that. Anyway, unless everything is going as planned he has no idea what to do. He didn't even want me to call you. I had to wait for him to go up to bed."

The more his mother went on, the more clearly Tom saw where she was headed. He *tried* to head her off ("Aunt Molly. How is she?" he asked. Then: "Hey, did Dad ever give in and get fitted for new glasses?"), but it was hopeless; she still popped the question. Seeing as what had happened had upset them all so, and seeing as his presence was always such a positive influence on Bud, couldn't he possibly alter his plans and make one more visit home?

"Before Cali*fornia*," she said, pronouncing it too carefully as she did these days, and brought to mind 'fornicate' and the disdain 'California' and 'fornicate' shared for her.

"But, Mother..." he skipped the baloney regarding his positive influence and reminded her that he had been home over Labor Day, just three short weeks before. He also reminded her that his severance pay ran out this month so that it was very important that he resettle as soon as possible (now that he had decided he was going to, that is) and find himself another job.

But none of it did any good.

"Just for a day or two?" she pressed.

"All right. It's a waste of time. I've told you what you ought to do. Furthermore, I don't see how my being there will make a bit of difference. But all right," he said, giving in.

"If it's a problem, Tom..." she said.

"No no," he said. This *was* his mother, he reminded himself, and Bud *was* his brother. "Just let me see what I can arrange. I'll call you back first thing tomorrow."

But the next morning after Tom had changed his plane reservation, he dialed his sister, Betty, the oldest. Six years ago Betty had married an air force pilot and, in a move Tom recognized as ingenious only later, split to Texas to raise her family.

Thus Betty was indisputably unavailable. Her three small kids not only demanded that she stick close to home but that she leave the phone twice before Tom had a chance to tell her that—unbelievably—he was headed back home.

"Oh, Tom, I know," she said. "She called here last night, too."

"Two days. That's it! I'm going up on the bus on Friday, and I'm leaving for San Francisco out of Logan on Sunday."

"Well, whatever, I'm glad," Betty said. "All this craziness with Buddy is taking its toll. It will help, your being there. You don't think so, I know, but it will. You *are* the only one he'll talk to."

"Oh, Betty, now you sound like her! Bud doesn't talk to anybody. All he does is listen to his tapes and practice that damn guitar. He's as polite as the rest of us. If you ask him a question, he answers. But he doesn't *talk* to anybody. And besides…Betty? Betty?"

"I'm back, Tom. Sorry," she said. "Luther was playing with the toaster oven."

"And besides, you know as well as I do that when I'm home he's never there. Or if he is, he's upstairs sleeping. Betty, you should see his room. And he's in another damn garage band. Did she tell you what this one is called?"

"Luther! Sorry, Tom. What?"

"'The Blazing Hairdos'? 'The Burning Hairdos'? Something like that."

"Anyway," Betty said, "it must be tough, Tom, to be, you know, the one who's stuck at home. There was a segment on "Lifetime" the other day. There's one in every family, they said, only usually, according to their panel, it's not the middle child, Tom, it's the youngest. And what I mean by the way is that you're the smart one in the family. At least you'll know what to do."

"What do you mean I'll know what to do?"

But suddenly there was a crash in the background and Betty had to go.

"Look, Tom," she said before she hung up, "you just let me know if you think I should fly home. Because I will, of course. If you think it's necessary. I'd have to drag along the kids, I suppose. But I could…I mean, I would!"

Would she? It was hard not to wonder. Perhaps if he'd been sure it wouldn't threaten to drag out his visit and work even further toward upsetting his plan, Tom would have called her on this. But for now he just told her what the both of them felt sure of: that by the time he even got home everything would have settled back to normal...Bud's latest infraction would be completely forgotten.

Just like the time his mother got up early one morning and found Bud in the upstairs shower, not alone, of course, but with some girl. Or the night when after supper Bud had ignored his mother's pleas and set out to walk the six miles to town just as a blizzard was whipping up. And then didn't return, *or* call, all night.

On both those particular occasions when Tom came home from work the next day, he could hear his phone ringing as soon as he came up out of the subway station and started down his block. But by the time the weekend rolled around and he had shown up (as promised) at home, the incidents which had had his mother in tears ("All I want is a little respect. Now, Tom, tell me, is that asking too much?") weren't even so much as mentioned.

In short: these episodes *always* fizzled. And nothing ever changed.

His coming was the important thing, and so if he was careful and played it right, he reminded himself once more, this could be a simple painless visit. There was no use letting it rile him. He would do whatever his mother wanted him to do, he would smooth everyone's feathers, and then he too would escape from this side of the country and his parents and his troublesome brother and all their problems once and for all, for good.

Thus bolstered, Tom dialed his parents and caught his mother just coming in from a white sale at Kimball's. Had everything blown over already?

"Oh, Tom, that's wonderful," she said. "It will mean so much to everybody!"

"Two days. That's it!" he warned. "I'm sorry, but it's the best I can do. I'll be on the bus on Friday afternoon, and I'm booked on a flight out of Logan first thing Sunday morning!"

~

Tom had a theory that no matter what he did, he could never—for some at least—do wrong. If he was a serial killer, for heaven's sake, and he was finally caught red-handed one morning while speeding home to change for work, *in spite of* the body lumped in his backseat and the bloody murder weapons wrapped in a raincoat and stuffed in his trunk, Tom was sure that when the media flooded his hometown people would still say *Tom? What, are you crazy? Tom?? Come on. No way!* And say it *so convincingly* that eventually even the investigators would agree. They'd let him off. With an apology. He'd go scot free.

Ever since a kid, Tom had always been treated this way. He had been the "good" son, whatever that meant. For reasons if he'd ever known he'd forgotten, he had been the one that not only his mother had relied on to help keep Bud in line, but all of the neighborhood mothers—Mrs. Ryan, Mrs. Sanders, even the ordinarily unfriendly Mrs. Orff—had relied on as well. If *Tom* was going to spend the night on the beach or go fishing off Badger's Island, then, all right, their sons could too. Tom—well-mannered, responsible Tom—*he* wouldn't get into trouble. And by his influence perhaps their sons wouldn't either.

And though all of that was a long time ago, of course, even now, years later, it was a reputation Tom still had not shaken. When Tom was home in response to one of his mother's calls and was out in the yard, say, raking up leaves, it still wasn't unusual for these neighborhood mothers to suddenly appear drying their hands on their kitchen towels to count on him again as they had counted on him then.

"Tom! You're home! For good?" they'd first ask. And then, when he had told them it was just for a few days to help his parents through the most recent Bud crisis, they'd confide (at length) the latest ways in which their sons had let them down.

And to Tom, while they stood there talking, trying to make sense out of whatever had happened (divorce was big these days, as was defaulting on car loans for some reason), it was as if what they were actually saying was that everything had all gone wrong on the very day he had decided to leave town. As if at least part of the blame for these filial disappointments was, in some way, somehow, his.

"So, couldn't you give him a call while you're here?" they would say. "*You* could knock some sense into him, I bet. You've done it before, Tom. Yes, you have. And Lord knows, *I* can't!"

As if his own mother's pleas weren't enough!

And when (oh when, oh when) had he ever knocked any sense into anybody ever before?

This reputation, then, was a burden. It was a burden that Tom had longed to get rid of when in Nedick's in Times Square one evening shortly after his last trip home—following an afternoon filled with a double feature at a movie house across the street—Tom looked at the teenage runaways meandering through the crowd outside and finally thought he saw how. Hair still matted, just off the bus, in their jeans and their sturdiest shoes and with their backpacks strapped high on their shoulders, they were looking at the lights spread out overhead with an expression that belied their bedraggled appearance and meant to Tom, too, that for one thing anyway each of them could surely be proud: rough times lay ahead, but they *had* managed, for the time being at least, to up and ditch their families!

Tom made his list right then on the back of his Nedick's napkin. FREEDOM went at the top—this meant a new home far away and a telephone number he'd make sure was not listed—and just below it BRAND NEW START.

He'd decided before he'd even finished his hot dog that night that he would pack up his old belongings and give all of them, everything, to Goodwill. He'd begin his new life on the west coast *from scratch.*

This was the plan Tom had made.

And indeed, on the very day he made the deal with his mother ("Two days! That's it! No more!"), when his apartment was completely empty, it was a plan that was still so simple and perfect (he would arrive in San Francisco with the clothes on his back and his overnight bag and nothing else whatsoever!) it made the prospect of his last trip home if not exactly something to look forward to, well, almost bearable.

But then came the call that toppled everything.

It was early the following morning when the phone rang once more.

It was (no surprise) Tom's mother. She told him that when she had gone upstairs to wake Bud after she had spoken to him about his new travel plans yesterday, she had gotten the shock of her life. Are you ready for this? she kept on saying. (Two or three times she said it at least!) Bud had shaved his head.

"Tom, you should have seen him!" she said. "All of that beautiful, gorgeous hair. He had your father's hair, you know. Or the hair your father *used* to have. Well, no more," she said, disgusted, "and it's an absolute crime, I tell you. All of it, Tom, was gone. He looked like a Holocaust victim. Or a cancer patient. Take your pick.

"But, Tom," she said, "remind me, will you? What time does your bus get in?"

Tom, taken aback by the quick change of subject, simply recited the scheduled arrival.

"That's when I thought it was," she said, "but I figured it was worth a quick call to make sure. So," she said, apparently finished, "so I guess we'll see you then!"

"*Wait!* Bud?" Tom ventured, before his mother had a chance to hang up. "What happened after you found him, mother?"

"Oh. Well, I told him if he left the house—I mean, looking like that! Can you imagine! *ha!*—he could very well not come back. Then I realized that I wasn't being very reasonable. Not to mention very smart. I mean we'd be stuck together here for weeks. So I went into the front hall closet and I dug out one of your father's old red flannel hunting caps, and I told him that if he left the house *without wearing a hat* he could very well not come back."

This relaxed Tom a little. This sounded like his mother. And, after all, she had threatened to kick his brother out of the house twice a week for the past ten years. But he still wasn't sure why she hadn't called yesterday when all of this had supposedly happened. And now the silence on the other end...this too, seemed to Tom a bad sign.

"*And?*" he probed uneasily.

"And he said 'Like hell!' and walked right out the front door and up the street, whistling his heart out. Can you believe it? As bald as a baby and the dummy, he couldn't have cared less."

When his mother was silent once more, Tom knew that something was wrong. "*So*, Mother. *Go on.*"

"So, like I said, I couldn't positively remember whether the bus from New York City got in at *two*-forty-five or *three*-forty-five."

"Mother, are you all right?" Tom asked. If he knew anything he knew that this was the sort of behavior that could put her in bed for weeks. (The pierced ear had done it for two! And the tattoo—three-and-a half!)

"Well, sure, I'm fine," she said, in a clear, uncomplicated voice.

"Well, then," he said, now really flustered, "Mother, is Bud all right?"

"Bud? How should I know? He left, I told you." Then, finally, it all spilled out:

"Tom, you were right," she said, "'Kick him out!' Remember? 'Stop catering!' You were absolutely right. But what you didn't tell me was how easy it would be. After he'd gone,

I lugged all of his belongings out to the driveway—all of his tapes and all of his stereo equipment, all of his *Creme* magazines and all of his old baseball trophies, all of those godawful tattered clothes he insisted on always wearing, all of his sheet music and all of his posters, Alice Cooper! Ozzy Osbourne! Iggy Pop! What kinds of names are those anyway, Tom?—and I dumped everything in a great big pile. Only neatly, of course," she added, "so that your father who was up at Buckminster Chapel—one of his old customers at the shoe store passed away—could get the car into the garage when he got back. Then I went around the house and I locked all the doors."

"Dad. Is Dad there?" Tom asked, chilled by his mother's news. "Let me speak to him for a minute, please?"

"*Ty*pically," she explained, ignoring him, "your brother didn't take his keys. Then I went directly down to the cellar to the freezer and I took out a couple of steaks for dinner. The short of it, your father and I had a nice quiet meal, and then afterwards we played cards until midnight. I can't tell you how wonderful it was. Can you believe it? When was the last time your father and I played cards? We played gin, but when you get home—tomorrow, Tom, we can hardly wait!—the three of us, just the three of us, we'll play hearts. Like old times!" she said, excited. Then:

"He's gone, Tom. Finally! And good riddance! All of his things that I left in the driveway, he must have had that Owen help him retrieve them with his van. It was all gone when we got up this morning.

"Tom? Are you there, Tom? *Tom?*"

"I'm here," he answered, weak.

"I did it for me, Tom," she said, "and I did it for you. I did it for your sister and her husband and their kids, though God knows we never see them anymore. I did it for your father!" she announced proudly. "And, Tom, let's all of us hope to God we never set eyes on him again!"

Right away he dialed Betty.

"Christ, she did it!" he said. "Who would've thought! She's locked him out!"

"I know, Tom," Betty said.

"She's banned him from the house forever! She said she doesn't want to set eyes on him ever *ever* again."

"Tom, I know," Betty said. "But don't worry. She is his mother."

After Betty had excused herself to drive her youngest to kindergym, Tom realized that Betty was right. Of course his mother would set eyes on Bud again. If it was his hair, his hair would grow back. And besides, where would Bud go? And how could Bud—*Bud!*—ever support himself. Even when he had a job he had spent his money so recklessly that he had been unable to afford to live anywhere but at home! Yes, he knew this as soon as Betty said it. All they had to do was wait.

But as he sits on the bus headed north, the commerce whizzing dizzily by, Tom is still uneasy. There is something else that's troubling him, and as far as Tom can figure it has to do with the change in his mother's voice during that last, unsettling call. A shift in focus. A minor adjustment in tone. He senses that something, though he's not sure what just yet, has suddenly, seriously changed.

He doesn't know that three weeks later there will be four postcards stuck to his parents' refrigerator, all of them written by Bud.

The first will arrive quite quickly, one of those freebies they tuck in next to the complimentary stationery, a boring shot of the hotel they are staying in, a Comfort Inn in Lorain, Ohio.

~

Hi everybody! Here we are on our way out west. So if you're worrying about me, don't, I'm fine!

~

The second will arrive a week later, another freebie from a Ramada in Sioux City, and the message, longer this time, will speak of a gig at a place called The Paradise Club ("They love us! They've booked us to play out the week!") and a scout from World Wide Records who will give them his card and tell them that when they "hit L.A. to be sure and hunt him up!"

He doesn't know there will be two more (from a Motel Six in Colorado Springs and a Howard Johnson's in Phoenix, Arizona) with more news of gigs in both those places, and happy, foot-stomping crowds. All four cards will be on proud display by the night his father will shoot the moon three hands straight and his mother, feigning insult, will fold.

He doesn't know that will also be the night he will excuse himself early, leaving his parents to make their tea by themselves, and go upstairs to get ready for bed. That will be the night he will have to be up at six the next morning to start work for a firm in Newmarket twenty-five minutes away. A temporary position for sure but, if all works out (according to the woman who will interview him at least), with a better than good possibility of eventually becoming permanent.

Tom knows none of this yet. And though he does his best to forget what his mother has done and concentrate on his slam-dunk plan (*his* getaway will be lasting and neat, a clean sharp break!), his uneasiness forces him to change his seat twice before the bus finally pulls into the familiar town square and he spots his parents' car and sees its driver's side fling open.

His mother has just had her hair done, another ominous sign.

He isn't as smart as they think he is, though. He should never have gotten on that bus. But he did, and so, when he clambers off, everything he owns in the world slung over his left shoulder, his mother throws her arms out to welcome him home—her wayward, youngest son.

The Recovery

THE MORNING AFTER her recovery she hops out of bed. Gets dressed. Starts right in cleaning the house.

There are some things you should know:

This was not a short illness;

The house hasn't been cleaned properly in years;

Two weeks ago the husband went to see a realtor about selling it.

I know exactly what you're going through, the realtor said. A tiny little man in a pink jersey, with a bright red face. He was sitting on the front of his desk, his hands wedged under his thighs. I lost my wife to lung cancer last year.

The husband was sitting in a chair just below him, fiddling with a "Happy Homes" pencil cup. There was also a "Happy Homes" blotter and a "Happy Homes" desk calendar, all in matching leather laid out on the realtor's huge desk.

Oh, it's not that, the husband said. There's nothing wrong with her really.

Oh, the realtor said, puzzled.

There's just no way I can take care of it, the husband said. Not with her and my business to take care of, too. Not at fifty-nine. That's what I've decided. No more.

Of course there isn't, the realtor said, crossing his legs. You've got the right idea. Sell. Put a little money in the bank.

Hire one of those live-in nurses if you want to. Get an apartment. By the way, have you looked into condominiums?

I wrote to my son at school, and he agrees.

Of course.

But I still can't help thinking, the husband went on. Can you imagine what it must be like, living in a room for twelve years, then suddenly being told you're moving out? I haven't been able to tell her just yet. No guessing what complications she'll come down with when I do. She's bound to come down with something.

Don't worry about it, the realtor said. You're making it too hard on yourself. My wife was in a damn hospital bed in our living room for three years. *I* should know. Sell. For chrissakes. You deserve to.

❧

The husband put the house on the market.

The realtor started showing it the next day.

From two to four in the afternoon.

That's the time, the husband said, she's sure to be asleep. She takes her nap from two to four. Puts in her ear plugs. Turns on the humidifier. God knows I can never get her on the phone. Don't worry about waking her up.

❧

Four days ago the realtor showed the house to a young couple from Minnesota. The man had just been hired by a law firm downtown. The woman was seven months pregnant. She glided from one room to the other as gracefully as a ship in full sail. They ignored the dishes stacked in the sink, the dust like velvet coverlets on the mantles, the Kleenex balled on the bathroom counter, the smell of antiseptic all through the house. They said, Our feet can't look at many more places. They said, As-a-matter-of-fact, this is the last house we want to set our eyes on in forty years. They didn't even ask to make special arrangements to see the master bedroom.

The husband took out his checkbook. We'll take it.

So:

The son's come home from college, in the Midwest, to collect his things.

The young couple's back in Minnesota packing all they own into a U-Haul.

The husband still hasn't told his wife.

Last night she made an amazing recovery.

She just walked into the kitchen after they'd started eating.

Ten minutes earlier she'd have rolled her head to the other side of the pillow, said she couldn't touch a thing (so they hadn't even fixed her a tray), and now she just walked into the kitchen, taking them by surprise, and said to the husband:

When you called me from Presque Isle and said if I didn't come up you were coming down, your mother had a hissy fit.... Do you remember?

Just walked in remembering these ancient events. Biting open a bobby pin. Nailing a strand of hair behind her ear.

They watched her, the husband and son, very carefully.

Do you remember the place we had? she said. Remember when you got your hip boots down from the attic to go fishing? When you put them on to show me how they looked and in one there was a whole nest of mice! Remember that?

They could tell she was thinking hard, trying to remember what they did next. She was rummaging through the cupboards. She stopped for a minute. Did we get the broom?

She found the plates, slid one out from the bottom.

Yes. That's right, she said. We got the broom. One of the mice got stuck behind the refrigerator. Must have been ten of them scattered over your lap, remember? How about the time we took your mother's car up after Christmas! God, I'll never forget that. I dropped you off at the garage on Portland and you said go ahead I'll be right along and your mother's car broke down on that godawful Route 12 in the middle of nowhere and when I got out and opened the hood there was all that smoke coming out of the engine so I threw snow on it until it stopped and then got in and just sat there with all the doors locked, for an hour and a half! The truck wasn't ready yet. *Remember that?*

She sat down with the both of them at the kitchen table. She had on her long, oatmeal-colored corduroy bathrobe. The one with the big scalloped collar. The one she usually wore only on holidays, because those were the only times they were used to seeing her out of bed.

I think I'll eat something after all, she said. Flattening her hands on either side of the plate she'd set on her placemat. Silverware! she suddenly said, holding up a finger, jumping up after it.

How…how do you feel? the husband said, finally, when she'd found the silverware drawer and was making a ruckus looking through it.

Oh, she said, her back bent to them. Where are the knives? Here they are. I feel fine.

~

She did the dishes afterward. She insisted. She sat up with them in the den and watched Johnny Carson. The husband got them all a bowl of ice cream. It was nice. Real nice. They could hardly believe it. But both of them were sure it was a fluke. She talked about cleaning in the morning, but neither one would've bet a quarter even then that they would have seen her set a foot out of bed.

~

When the son gets up and finds her hustling up the cellar stairs, the first thing he says is My God. He almost doesn't recognize her in slacks and a blouse and a pair of sneakers.

He's still in his pajamas.

My God, he says. Be careful.

Carry up those boxes I set aside for the Goodwill, will you? she says full of energy, brushing past him, muttering about starting on the floors.

My God, he says, and lumbers down the stairs, holding up his pajamas. And in the cellar sure enough he finds the boxes piled neatly on the floor next to the water heater. On top of one of them is an old pair of skates. The leather on the toes chipped like tree bark. He carries everything, in a state of shock, up to the front porch.

The skates, it turns out, belong to his father. Who on any other day would've waved them into the garbage heap, but who is so happy with his wife's sudden recovery (when he woke up this morning she was sitting on the edge of her bed, tying double-knots into her sneakers) he retrieves them before the Goodwill truck picks them up.

You've got to tell her! the son says for the umpteenth time that morning. He is sitting on the wooden bench that's provided by the city. Holding one leg out, then the other. Tugging on his lacings, hooking them tighter. He hasn't been on ice skates since a fifth-grade outing. She's recovered! She should know you've sold the house. After all!

The husband's out on the pond doing half-turns, squiggling off backwards along the ice.

She's home cleaning right now! the son says. She was getting ready to put the venetian blinds in the bathtub when we left! You know as well as I do you better tell her right away, or when you do it's going to knock her flat on her back. You know how delicate she can be. Put her right back in bed for another twelve years if you're not careful. When's that couple getting here?

The husband's on the other side of the pond. He puts his hand up behind his ear, aims it toward the son.

THE COUPLE FROM MINNESOTA. WHEN ARE THEY COMING?

THURSDAY. COME ON OUT. IT'S BEAUTIFUL!

THIS THURSDAY? the son yells.

The husband smiles, aims his ear again.

They're coming in *four* days? the son says, skating towards him. Blowing into his mittens, beating his chest against the cold.

The couple from Minnesota? Uh-huh.

You've got to be out in *four* days?

No. Wait. No, I guess it's three, the husband says, skating in a circle around the son. I found an apartment at Edgewood Manor. The movers are coming on Wednesday. Didn't I tell you? He begins tacking around the edge of the pond.

Three days? the son says.

But the husband's bent forward, he's really begun to move. Digging with his blades. Swinging his arms underneath him. Swiping the ice now and then with his hands.

OKAY, the son yells. IF YOU'RE NOT WORRIED, I'M NOT WORRIED. I'LL BE BACK AT SCHOOL BY WEDNESDAY MORNING ANYWAY! And then he stands in the middle of the ice, just watching him. Still lapping around the pond, crossing one foot over in front of the other. He never even knew that his father could skate! He knew he could cook and clean house, paint signs, which is his job, but....

HEY, he yells. *BOBBY ORR.* WHERE'D YOU LEARN TO DO ALL THAT FANCY STUFF?

When I was a boy, the husband says. I played hockey. He's skating toward him, unbending his knees, straightening up. He stops suddenly, on a dime, shaving the ice. As if he has a stick he hunches over, guards all sides. He brings his arms up, slaps down murderously. He makes a shot.

Tomorrow, she says, pulling her apron off and leaving it on the counter, sitting down at the table in front of a platter full of ham steaks, I want us to take a ride up to Arundel. If the weather isn't bad. Before Davy has to head back out west. Won't that be nice? We can take the back roads. I'll show you where I grew up!

Besides the ham there's a sticky slice of pineapple on each piece, a maraschino cherry planted in the middle. There's hubbard squash, which has come out a little too watery, a pile of mashed potatoes, a mite burned, so no one mentions it, wax beans from a can, and a loaf of bread, home-made, which looks fine.

Sure. Tomorrow we'll take a ride up through Maine! the husband says. Delighted with his wife's first cooking attempt in years. Noticing there are candles on the table.

After the meal, after Jell-O, the husband, full to his gills, settles back into his chair and goes to town on his teeth with a match cover.

The son tells them what's been doing out at school. What courses he's been taking. How he likes the place he's living. About his crazy landlord fixing the porch roof right outside his window. Talking to him continually through the screen so he can't get any work done.

How's it different out there? I mean the land? the husband says, examining his match cover for a fresher edge.

The son muses a minute, his mouth full of Jell-O. It's flat he finally says, dropping his jaw, speaking from the roof of his mouth. A lot flatter than here, he says. Like for one thing, the roads are much straighter. Much straighter.

Well, she says, taking her napkin off her lap. Did you both have enough? Wait till you see what I'm going to cook for you tomorrow night! I found an old recipe, a favorite of your father's, in your grandmother's cookbook, she says to the son.

We'll do the dishes! the husband says. You just go on in the den and watch a little television.

I can't believe it, he says, collecting the plates. It's a miracle. Do you think it will last?

I hope so, the son says.

They look at one another in their reflection in the window in front of them.

I hope so too, the husband says, smiling, wrapping the dish towel around his wrist. Flicking it in the air, he begins to shuffle in a crazy dance across the kitchen floor.

What's going on out here? she says, standing in the doorway, creasing the evening paper against her hip.

We're doing the dishes, the husband says, settling down. And when they finish he goes into the den with his wife, and the son goes up to his room to pack boxes.

I still don't think this is the place, she says. There must be another one.

They're at the cemetery in Arundel, looking for her Aunt Nell's grave. I can remember having our picnics on a hill. Every Fourth of July she brought us kids down in the cow buggy, and we spent the day. But it was on a hill. There's no hill here.

No hills here, the son says, sitting in the open car door with his legs out, shaking his head when she looks at him.

Think they have two cemeteries? the husband says, doubtfully. Looks like a pretty dinky town to me.

Well, she says, maybe this *is* it. It's been a long time after all. Maybe the ground's settled, I don't know. Come on. Look for Franklin Hathaway. That was Aunt Nell's husband's name. She's beside him.

The three of them split up and search.

Maybe it wasn't Arundel, she says back at the car after no luck. Maybe it was Acton? No. I don't think it was Acton. Drive out slowly, she says. One last look.

Oh well, she says, as they pass under the arch at the gate, turning around, settling in her seat.

But they're out on the main road just a minute when they come to another. This one, sure enough, is on a hill.

I'll be damned, the husband says.

Here it is! she says. This is it. I knew it was on a hill. She's run up ahead already and found the stone. After all these years, here it is! she says. We used to lay our blankets out right here. See, Hathaway, she says as the both of them come around to where they can read it. Franklin Hathaway. His wife, Cornelia. Aunt Nell. I never knew Uncle Franklin, he died before I was born, she says. But good-old Aunt Nell. Sometime during the afternoon she used to grab onto each one of us, stand us right here in front holding us by the shoulders and say, Now, Frank, this is Katherine. Hasn't she *grown?* she'd say, smoothing our hair. Can you believe it, Frank? she'd say, shaking our shoulders, Katherine, can you believe it, is *eight.*

Not a bad location, the husband says, after catching his breath.

It's a funny-looking cemetery. No wider a strip of land than if it had been cleared for some power lines. The headstones are scattered in uneven rows.

The wife steps back to get a good look, then gets down on her hands and knees and pulls out some stubble that's grown up in front.

Isn't that Mount Chocorua over there? the husband says, pointing to a low range of hills in the distance. No, he says, it couldn't be. Mount Chocorua's off to the west.

They stand on the hill for a while. Until a truck barrels by on the road below.

Well, the husband says, putting his arm around his wife. You did real well, Katie, just remembering after all these years.

~

It's Tuesday. The son has to head back to school on the bus. The wife's packed him sandwiches, some fruit. Something she hasn't done for him since he was a little kid. He's embarrassed. She's sewn patches on a pair of his pants. Buttons on three of his shirts. She did his laundry, folded everything, the night before.

~

The husband still hasn't broken the news.

While they're driving the son downtown to catch the bus, it's as if he realizes the whole mess for the first time.

~

What if she gets sick again? he says to the son, touching his shoulder.

I don't know, the son says, taken by surprise. The husband coming up behind him so sudden in the drugstore, with that expression set on his face. I don't know. Look, she'll probably like the idea of a smaller place anyway. Edgewood Manor, you said? He opens his jacket and puts the bus ticket the clerk has just given him into his pocket. That's nice.

They head down the aisle, back toward the front of the store.

My room's all cleaned out, the son says. Except for a couple of boxes. I left some posters on the walls. Coat hangers and junk in the closet. You can throw all that stuff out if you want to. Holding the door for his father, I've gone all through it, he says. There's nothing there that I want.

You're right, the husband says as the son follows him out the door. After you leave I've got to tell her. That's all.

When he's helping the son load his trunk underneath the bus:

After you leave, I'll just say, Katie, I sold the house.

~

The temperature board in front of the bank says twelve degrees. When she sees them coming, her door opens, she hops out.

I'm sure the bus'll be leaving in a minute. You don't have to wait, the son says.

What do you mean? she says. Of course we'll wait.

They stand by the car, leaning against the hood, after the son has boarded the bus. Wait for the driver who's in the drugstore digging for change to buy gum.

She has her arms folded high on her chest. Her parka, you'd notice right off, is way too big for her. While she's shading her eyes trying to find which one is his window, you can hardly see her hand, the sleeves are so long. Her stocking cap has slipped down her brow.

There he is! she says, nudging her husband, pointing him out, vigorously waving her whole arm.

The husband is standing next to her, rocking on his feet. Whistling so that vapor puffs out his mouth. When she nudges him, he stops. He waves. As if nothing in the world could ever bother him. He keeps glancing at the downtown traffic. Looks at the bus, in fact, only when he has to. At the son who's miles away already behind the window's tinted glass.

When the bus has left, they get into the car.

The husband scrubs his hands together, adjusts the heater.

She's on the passenger side, her arms huddled between her knees. She shudders up to her shoulders when she feels the blower kick on.

He has his arm up on the back of the car seat, he's backing out, waiting for a gap in the Tuesday morning traffic. All of a sudden he says, I wouldn't be surprised if when we get up tomorrow morning there's a foot of snow on the ground. Not at all, he says. Glancing at the traffic, glancing at his wife. I wouldn't be surprised at all, would you?

The Disappearance

THE TRAFfiC CIRCLE in Lee was deserted. The marquee at the Dover Drive-In flickered out as they passed. Grace stirred in the backseat.

"Where are we?" she said. "Are we there?"

"Not yet," Warren said, "but almost."

They passed a shopping center sprawled on the outskirts of town. Green SALE banners curled in the breeze. "*What's that? That's new,*" Warren said. "That used to be the Frink farm," he said, re-settling. They hit a pothole, the both of them bounced and Grace let out a scream in the back. "But that's the only thing so far that's changed."

"What time is it?" moaned Grace, sitting up.

Warren glanced at his watch. "Twelve-thirty." He swerved for a cat.

"Twelve-thirty!" She held the back of his seat for support. "Warren, do you think they'll be up?"

"Sure they'll be up. I told them on the postcard we'd be late."

"If they got it."

"They got it."

"Well throw me my purse then," she said, reluctantly. "And turn that mirror a little this way, will you please?"

"Not only that, I will turn on the light."

Grace just looked at him, her hair mashed flat on one side. She uncapped her lipstick. She put some on.

"I just wonder," she said, "about the phone. Awful funny

they haven't answered it when you've called. I don't see how you can be so sure they'll be home if they haven't answered their phone. How do you know they haven't gone away?"

"Because I told you, they never go anywhere. They love staying right here at home. Neither one of them's been out of town, I don't think, since they went to Hampton Beach on their honeymoon forty-five years ago, for one night."

"Yes, but Warren, what's it been? Since you ran away, I mean. Ten years? You haven't seen them, even talked to them in ten years."

"Look. My father once let a neighbor cheat him on his boundary because he didn't want to go to Concord to court. Don't worry. They'll be there," he said. He looked at her. She was pressing her lips. "The phone must just be out of order."

"Right. But, Warren," she dropped the tube in her purse, "for *three days*?"

They passed the state liquor store. The Drop Anchor Motel. Warren told Grace their motto: BERTH WITH US FOR THE NIGHT. They passed Mike's Marina and the dry-docked pleasure boats, their hulls looming like giant pelicans alongside the road. They crossed the General George Donovan Bridge. The New Hampshire cow fields stretched into darkness on each side.

"There, look. I told you they'd be up."

"Is that it?"

"That's it," Warren said, turning onto the short dirt drive.

The large, square farmhouse in front of them was lit up inside like a lantern.

"How do I look?" Grace asked, suddenly nervous. "I know what I feel like. Like someone who was invited but couldn't come."

"Let me see. You look fine," Warren said.

"Christ. You should have told them." She was smoothing her skirt.

"If I'd told them there wouldn't have been *any* surprise."

"Warren, I need a cigarette. Drive around."

"I can't. We're here!" he said. Then, "Don't worry." He reached over the seat and patted her leg. "They won't eat us." He smiled. He hopped out of the car. "Let's go."

But Mr. and Mrs. Race weren't home.

"They couldn't have gone out. They never go out." Warren and Grace were standing in the well-lit front hall. Warren had just searched the upstairs. To Grace, "You wait here a minute, I'm going outside to look around."

"It's twelve-thirty! What would they be doing outside?"

But already Warren had left.

Grace went into the living room. She lit her cigarette. She nosed around.

It was a big room, one whole corner of the house, and what was in it was very neatly laid out. She admired the floorboards that pitched every which way from age; the braided rugs; the brick fireplace; the Duncan Phyfe hutch. There was none of the clutter, Grace noticed, that one expects with living years in one place. She and Warren had only lived in their apartment in Detroit for three weeks, but when they had decided to make the move back east already their apartment had been a mess.

When she heard Warren come back in from outside she was examining a photograph from the mantle.

"Hey, Warren, this must be you when you were in high school, huh?" He had a crewcut and wore a long thin black tie. She spewed smoke. She set it back. "Ha! You were cute!"

She could hear Warren in the back of the house, rummaging through the kitchen cabinets.

"Hey, Warren, I'd give anything for this fireplace. How old is it, anyway?" she asked. "A hundred? Two hundred? I wouldn't be surprised—

"Hey, Warren, you know," she said. "I've never heard anything like it. When people go out around here do they always leave all their doors unlocked? I can see the sense to leaving on a light, but every single one? If you ask me, it's spooky," she said. She stopped.

"Warren? That's you, isn't it? — *Warren?*"

"What?"

"Warren! God. Why didn't you answer? What are you doing out there, anyway?" she said, heading across the hall toward the kitchen.

"Looking for the damn phone book."

"Does the phone work?"

"Yes."

"Thought so," she said, to herself.

Warren was scanning the kitchen on all sides.

"Warren, I need an ash tray," she said. "Never mind." She headed for the sink. The column of water burst forth with such force it blew the stub right out of her hand.

"Ah!" Warren said suddenly, remembering. He pulled the phone book off the refrigerator and started rifling through its pages.

"Now who are you calling at this hour?" Grace asked.

"The police." Warren struggled with the cord.

"The po*lice?* You didn't—Warren," she said. "You didn't find anything out there. Did you?"

In no time two cruisers arrived. The whole countryside pulsed with blue light. Warren met the patrolmen in front and directed them straightaway to his find. The patrolmen were as baffled as he. They examined it very closely with their flashlights. *"Has anyone been burning any leaves?"* But it was April, not a leaf-burning month. And on this side of the property, no trees! They split up; searched the house, searched the barn. After a spell they returned empty handed. There were no bodies. There was no weapon. No blood. Just a deep, star-strewn sky, and an almost perfectly round black circle burnt into the south parcel of the front lawn. They all stood there. They walked around it. They bent over and touched it. But either no one had the courage to say a thing, or all were afraid to, thinking one of the others might laugh. Until one of the patrolmen went to his cruiser to report back. Then Grace got the tape measure from Mrs. Race's sewing basket in the den. They measured it across the middle, though none of them knew exactly what for. It was thirty-six-and-three-quarters feet wide.

Boxford County buzzed. Not since Rollie Emerton, who managed a filling station downtown, was a finalist as a youngster in the Pitch, Punt, and Throw, had Boxford County—outside of an occasional score as THE NATION'S COLD SPOT—made such a mark for itself in the news.

When the dispatch left the office of the town paper, UPI wired back:

SEND 1,000 WORDS. PLUS PIX!

The dinner dishes in their drying rack by the sink, Tuesday's paper open in Mr. Race's easy chair in the den, Mrs. Race's apron in a clump on the kitchen counter—as if Mr. Race had gotten up to answer the door and Mrs. Race, curious who it was, had gone behind—were soon in all the dailies across the state. Along with the pictures of the mysterious black circle branded indisputably on the lawn.

The old couple watched it in color on a Boston newscast that night. The tipsy, hand-shot footage of the house. Of Warren beside the trellis on the porch, reading a statement ("*just in case*," he said, "the abductors might be watching") pleading for his parents' return.

"Shh," the old man said. "*Shhhh!*"

Though the old woman, who'd just come in, wasn't making a peep.

"Well, we did it," he said afterwards, lying back. Shutting

the set off with the remote control. "I told you not to worry, it'd work." He set the small control box on his stomach. He cracked his wrists. "We did it! We did it! We did it!" he said. He was so delighted he could have jumped up and danced.

The old woman, though, couldn't keep quiet any more. "I feel guilty already," she said.

"What? Don't say it," the old man said. He pressed a button, the set flipped back on. He was lying in his stocking feet on one of the suite's two huge beds. "Don't even say it," he said.

"I can't help it. You heard what he said. 'On behalf of me and my wife.' That girl behind him, with the little hat on, was his wife!" The old woman let her arms hang limp from her chair. She had her coat on, pea-green, with big square buttons. It was the same coat she had had when they were married, but it was only the fifth time she had worn it in her life.

"Don't say it. Don't *say* it," the old man said. "We promised *no guilt*, remember?" He pressed the button that increased the sound, till it was blasting, to block her out.

"But who would have ever thought? Who would have ever thought?"

"STOP!" But it was no use, he could see. The old woman was in a world all her own.

"—First, that he'd come home after all these years? And second, that, without mentioning it, he'd bring a *wife?*"

The old woman had just come in on the hotel courtesy bus from downtown. She'd gone shopping. She was wearing a new scarf. She'd gotten her hair cut. She was all horsed up.

"Do you think maybe it means he's ready to settle down now?" she asked. "He's put on weight. He shaved that beard off. He had on a suit!"

"Don't be crazy," the old man said. "Can I believe my ears? No, I can't. Look, you can't teach an old dog new tricks."

"I wonder what her name is?" she pondered. Dreamily, she unknotted her scarf. "He didn't mention her name, I don't think."

The old man plugged up his ears.

"June! I'll bet it's June," she said. "Did you see that hat she had on, with the flap? I bet I saw ten of those hats today. They're attractive, I think, don't you? Evidently, they're very in style." The old woman tucked her scarf in her purse. "Yes, June," she said, "something simple. She really looked awfully nice."

The old man unplugged his ear while he spoke: "It's too late. Do you hear me?" he screamed. "We decided that if he ever came back we would leave. He came. We left. We can't go slinking back now!"

The old woman looked at him.

He plugged up his ears.

"But couldn't we call?" she said.

Unplugging, "They'll look for us!" he said.

The old woman set her purse on the floor beside her. "You're right," she said, "I guess not."

"What?"

"NO WE CAN'T," she said. "YOU'RE RIGHT. I GUESS NOT."

The old man dropped his arms, caught his breath. "Well now," he said, relieved. "Well now, that's more like it. And really," he turned the sound down on the television, "it really is better this way. This way there's no chance either one of us will be disappointed." He cracked his wrists. "Ever again," he said, "right?"

"I guess so," the old woman sighed.

"Don't be silly. Right," the old man said. "Now, if you don't mind I would like to relax. Gunsmoke will be on in a minute."

They had never had a TV. Since they'd arrived at the airport earlier in the week, the old man had barely budged from the bed. Room service brought up his meals. When he went into the bathroom he held the door open with his foot.

"Now hand me that schedule, will you?" he said.

He shrugged. He looked at the clock. Understanding that he had a few minutes, he pointed to the bags at her feet. A pile of them, like a sand wall, stretched around. "You might as well show me the damage."

But all afternoon the woman had been worrying about something. This came back to her now and she jumped. "What if they discover the guernseys?" she said.

"Here we go again." The old man sat up. "They won't. The dealer who bought them said he was going to sell them in New York!"

"I mean, what if they discover they're gone?"

"Well of course they'll discover they're 'gone'. And when they discover they're 'gone' they'll just think the spacemen took off with them, too. We've been over all this already."

"All right, all right," she said, "don't get angry. It's just I'm not used to breaking the law."

"We haven't 'broken the law'! Christ, you make *me* nervous," he said. He felt weary, as if he'd been explaining all his life. "How have we 'broken the law'? We didn't steal a car to get here. We took the bus. We didn't rob a bank. We sold the cows. And good riddance. WE haven't done anything wrong, remember? You can't be arrested for burning a hole in your lawn! We're just going on a little vacation."

"And never coming back."

"That's right," he said, "that's right. But in a month we'll be totally forgotten. Mark my word. No one will even remember who we were."

The old woman thought about this for a minute. It was true she and Mr. Race weren't the best at communicating, but they both *had* agreed upon this. She thought and then, finally, she reached for the shopping bags at her feet. "Well," she said, taking a deep breath, "seeing as you were determined we couldn't bring a thing—and I will never forgive you for making me leave those wet dishes by the sink—I had to just about buy out the stores."

Excitedly, she told him what they were like. The long escalators carrying the people up up out of sight. The festivity; the noise; the thick crowds. The perfume counters galore, with all the salesladies in their make-up, and their jewelry and silk. "And the prices," she said, "the prices were horrendous. I had to keep reminding myself it was only this once. If only I had been able to bring my sewing machine," she said.

But really she was happy she couldn't. She unpacked the clothes, practically a new wardrobe for them both, and laid them with a flourish on the empty bed.

It was during this that the old man noticed for the first time that there was something unsettling about his wife. It took a minute for him to figure it out, and even then exactly what it was didn't quite click.

"Your hair? It's your hair. You did something to your hair!"

The old woman, who knew him, was taken aback. "I had it cut. You noticed. Do you like it?" she asked.

"Aren't you too old to have your hair cut?" he asked.

"No. I don't think so," she said. She was used to these comments by now. She chose to ignore it and continued right on.

"Go try those shorts on, you said you wanted some shorts," she said, slipping her coat on a hanger. *Walk*ing into the closet, it was so big. "Because if they need to be returned," she said muffled, "it's going to have to be first thing tomorrow."

The old man's ears perked. He hopped off the bed. "Don't tell me you've finally decided where you want to go?"

She reappeared, stood up straight. "Yes, I've decided," she announced.

"Praise the Lord! Hal-lelujah!" This time he didn't restrain himself, he did a jig.

The old woman washed her hands in one of the pink scalloped sinks. "I've decided I want to go to Palm Springs."

"Palm Springs! Palm Spr— Are you sure? That's a long ways off. Isn't it?" The old man was flustered. "I mean I think it's a long ways off. Isn't that the place contestants win trips to on those shows?"

"I suppose it is," she said. She was standing with her back to their patio, mindlessly toweling her hands. The lights atop the main air tower over her shoulder were twinkling brightly in the dusk. "But I guess if we're going to do this, we might as well do it up right. I stopped at the travel agency, that little travel agency yesterday in the lobby, and I picked up some of those fancy brochures. I was reading them on the bus coming home. There's a place there called The Gold Sands Motel. It's on a lake with a private beach. And there's the social center," she said, "right close by. So we can make a life, a new life, just for us. But the best thing," she sat with a thump on the bed, her legs flashing, "the best thing, it has monthly rates. And some of the units have their own kitchenettes! It's more than we planned on spending," she said, "but I guess maybe if we both find jobs, somehow, I guess, we'll get by."

"TV?"

"It has a TV."

The old man spun around, ecstatic, then stopped. "But are you sure? I mean really, you've got to be sure."

"I wouldn't have brought it up if I wasn't sure."

"All right, all right. It's fine with me. I don't care where we go, as long as we go." The old man was pacing the room. He clapped his hands together, loudly, once. "Good good. We can get out of here," he said. "At last. Good good. Palm Springs it is."

It was as if he realized all of a sudden how he looked.

"Where'd you get your hair done, anyway?" he said soberly, swinging his legs up one by one onto the bed.

The old woman dropped her hands in her lap. "I didn't have it done, I had it *cut*. Do you like it?"

"I said I liked it, didn't I?" he said. "Now, *shhh!*" He raised the sound. Matt Dillon came on.

...It's very difficult for me to imagine them 'up there'. I'm better at imagining them at the beach. We often went to the beach on Sundays when I was a kid. Headed off early in the morning, took a picnic lunch, which we ate right at noon, then left, to avoid the crowds.

I can imagine my father leaning up against our cooler reading the Sunday paper very clearly. He was quite a reader, my father. He read everything, even the ads. He would sit there, no matter how hot the day, in the same heavy work clothes he'd been wearing all week, and scour it from cover to cover.

Once in a while, if it was exceptionally hot, my father would roll up his pants, but never any higher than his shins. The general rule was he didn't even unlace his shoes.

In fact, there was a standing joke on this subject between us:

My mother, or I, would say, "Dad (even she called him 'Dad') aren't you going to wear your bathing suit today?" And either he, or my mother, or I would say "Can't. It's got a hole in the elbow!"

I can see my mother sitting on her towel just as clearly. (We never, that I can remember, brought a blanket. And we often sat a good deal apart.) My mother, she had a suit, but just one. Which she always, necessarily, wore. It was old, gray as I remember, and sewn from a heavy, blanket-like material which meant if she went into the water it would take the rest of the day to dry.

She wore a kerchief tied in two knots on her head, and she always sat perfectly straight. With her legs folded neatly underneath her, knitting something or other. My mother was a great knitter.

But if not at the beach, I'm imagining my parents in the gymnasium, at school. I was big on basketball for a while, before I ran away. I played on the A-team my senior year, and my parents, though not smart on going out, always came to the at-home games.

They sat in the same seats in the bleachers every time.

Together (in a crowd they always stuck together), not on the parents' side where all the parents always sat, but on the other, with all the kids. Alone, they never knew anybody, on the very tip-top row....

That time at the airport, before they had left, that wasn't the only time she saw her son on TV. She saw him again, a year and a half later. Caught him out of the corner of her eye when she was routing dust bunnies out from under the bed, on a panel show that just happened to be on. A discussion of UFOs. Evidently, he had written a book.

She thought it wise not to mention this to Mr. Race, who at the time was in his shorts and bow tie bagging groceries at a market down the street—he was happy, there was no use upsetting him, she thought—but she did think of looking this book up for herself.

"It's called, let's see, *The Disappearance*," she said, taking out the slip of paper on which she'd very carefully written it down. She followed the librarian across the ante-room toward the files. "I think it is a mystery," she said. "I don't know if that matters. If it helps."

She gathered from the librarian's attitude that it didn't. No matter what it was, it wasn't in their files. If she would like to, really wanted to, the librarian said, she could fill out a borrower's request card at Reference Services. Reference Services is one flight up.

"Oh no, that won't be necessary," Mrs. Race said. "But thank you, thank you anyway. Thank you very much."

And Mrs. Race, who was now Mrs. Bick (all the friends she'd met at the social center where she taught sewing classes called her June), was surprised to find, once outside, that it really wasn't necessary. She hardly minded not finding Warren's book at all. Granted, for the next few weeks she kept an eye out whenever she passed the book-rack at the supermarket, but this was mainly because she still had that fear, that fear of being someday found out. As far as she knew there weren't any photos they could have used, at least any that resembled them now (there had been a few in her top bureau drawer, but they were of them both on their honeymoon, on the boardwalk at Hampton Beach, and Lord knows no one would recognize them from those!), but they might have done a composite drawing, might they not?

All these worries, though, as the weeks carried on, as they went out to card parties, anniversaries and birthdays, baptisms and even a wedding—Gert Zideman married that nice, thin man who drove the carry-van weekdays from the center to the mall—worried Mrs. Race less and less. Until, with a gesture like the toss of a hand, Mrs. Bick casually gave them up.

In El's Feeling Sorry for My Mother's Old Boyfriends

WE'RE WAITING for our order in El's Fried Clams, a place I haven't been to in years. At one of the same wooden booths with the plum-colored tops. Under the same gray fishnets draped across the ceiling, with the same giant starfish, the same plastic lobsters, the same styrofoam, long-stemmed buoys. I say, "I see they haven't changed the decor."

My mother, shrugging out of her coat sleeves, laughs. "You can't squeeze in here any more in July and August. But in the off season it's still pretty nice."

"I've never been in here before in the winter, I don't think."

"Not unless you came home and I didn't know about it," she says. "They've only been open year round since last year." She unsnaps her rain hat, shakes the melted snow onto the floor, then lays the hat out delicately beside her to dry.

We sit back and look around. Outside the snowflakes are large and wet, so that they stick to the window shaped like a porthole beside us, dissolve, then jigger off.

I say, "I remember Steve wouldn't touch his fried clams. All he'd ever eat were his French fries, and drink Coke."

My mother smiles, poking her hairdo back into shape.

"How is Steve?" I ask. "Did he and Marjorie ever put that pool in their backyard?"

My older brother, Steve, works for an insurance company in Hartford and lives there with his wife and two kids.

Though there was a day when we came to El's all the time—my parents, Steve and I—it's been a while now since he and I have been back home together. I'm a problems expert for a computer firm in L.A., and this is my first visit east in a year.

"Oh, they put it in," she says, disgusted, "though I'll never understand who would want a pool in their backyard in *Hartford.* But Marjorie did evidently." She humphs. "So," she humphs again, "that was that."

We're sitting here in February just waiting for our clams when suddenly my mother does something strange with her eyes. They flare as if she's been poked with a spit, and Marjorie and her pool fly out the window.

"If I didn't know any better," she says in a low whisper, leaning forward, "I'd say that the man sitting in the corner behind you is Charlie Baxter's son." She signals toward a booth in the back. "It looks just like him," she says, and then goes under the table for her purse.

I say, "Who's Charlie Baxter?"

"Charlie Baxter. You know," she says. "I've told you about Charlie Baxter! One of the boys I went out with before your father." She takes a napkin from the dispenser and scrubs the lenses of her glasses, then unfolds them and puts them on. "That woman with him, it must be his wife." Her eyes flare again, into focus. "Holy Toledo. It looks just like him!"

She suddenly, nonchalantly, sits back. "Don't look now, he's looking," she warns.

She straightens the little sugar packets in their rack on the table between us and gradually zeroes back in. "Did you see them when we came in? *I* didn't. I thought we were the only ones here. You can look now," she says, "they're talking." She says, "He thought I was going to marry him."

"Mom, he looks twenty-five."

She laughs. "Not *him*, his father. Charlie Baxter. I never *said* I was going to marry him, but there was a misunderstanding. He definitely thought that I was. If only I could see him a little better."

I can't think of a thing my mother ever wanted and didn't get.

One of the young girls who took our order calls out a number, and the man slides out of his booth and heads to the counter for his clams.

As he passes our booth, my mother eyes him carefully, discreetly. "Same height. Same build," she says under her breath. She glances at him over the tops of her glasses. "A little heavier, but everyone's heavier these days."

"Was he in the car the time you were in that accident and broke your nose?" I'm referring to one of the stories that as kids Steve and I, for some reason, always loved for her to tell. Usually just before dinner when she was sitting in her apron at the set kitchen table, waiting for whatever was cooking to finish, reading the evening paper—when you couldn't imagine her in a car full of screaming kids weaving down some backwoods road.

"*No*," she says with a laugh, "that was when I was going with Franny Lindeman, in Exeter. This was after I had moved down here. When I was working at the radio station and boarding at your father's mother's." Then, remembering who she's talking to, "At *Nana's*. During the war. Just before your father came home."

I'm sure she has never mentioned Charlie Baxter before, but it doesn't seem worth arguing about. The young girl calls out another number, ours, and I get up to get our order.

"Want tartar sauce?" I call back to her from the counter.

Hardly looking at me, eyes still on Charlie, or his son, she nods.

It's my father's late night. He distributes tobacco for a company in Manchester and his territory is Eastern New Hampshire and Maine. On Mondays his route runs from Rochester to Milton, which means he doesn't get back to the house until eight. So Monday nights, when I'm home, my mother and I eat out.

"Just *like* him," she says, shaking her head, when I return with two clam boats, heaped. Having got even a better, longer look when I left her a clear view. "That's the Baxter nose or I'm a cat's meow." Distracted, she centers the boat on its plate.

"So it's him. So what? Aren't you going to take your glasses off?" I say, flicking open a napkin and digging in. I'm not used to my mother wearing glasses. Usually she only wears them at the movie. Or at hockey games, for example, when my brother and I were kids.

But she leaves them on, as if not hearing me. Though they mean she can't tell the salt from the pepper without holding them out at arm's length. Though they mean her eyes look a little too big for her head, and though of course they mean that for the rest of our meal the only things she can see really clearly are things that are set a ways off.

"He was overseas for eighteen months," she says after a pause of at least ninety seconds.

"Who?"

"Charlie Baxter! And then he came home on leave without telling me he was coming and went to Nana's and Nana told him I'd gone to the Hampton Beach Casino with some girlfriends, which luckily I had, and he came down there—he'd *just* gotten home, I bet his mother could have killed him—and came up behind me out on the dance floor and tapped me on the shoulder. Well I thought he was overseas. In a jungle somewhere. He'd sent me postcards. 'What are you doing here?' I said. 'I'm home on leave,' he said, 'surprise!' Surprise, all right. Oh, I was glad to see him, but it meant I had to dance with him the rest of the night.

"Aren't the clams *good?*" she says, only looking at them now for the first time, though they must look to her quite blurry. "You can't beat these clams, can you?" As if made hungry by the sudden recollection of her girlhood, she smooths out a napkin and eats.

"*Well?*"

"Well, what?" she says.

"What happened? Did he propose that night, or what?"

"Oh, not that night," she says with her mouth full. "But, *mmm*"—she waves her fork and takes her time before she swallows—"the end of his leave. He still had six months left and he was going to be stationed in Georgia or something. That's when he asked me to marry him. Three days before he went. He wanted me to go south with him, can you imagine?"

My mother eating with her glasses on really looks terribly strange. And again she stops talking just when she's caught my interest. She's eating to beat the band.

"So?"

"So, what?" she says.

"So, what did you say?"

"No." She gives a laugh and wipes her mouth with her napkin. "What did you think I said? Yes?" She laughs a little more. Then, "It's not funny, I guess, is it? There'd been a misunderstanding. I liked it here." She leans forward, chewing. "I certainly didn't want to run off to *Geor*gia."

"Mom, can you see me?" I ask.

"Of course I can see you," she says, looking over my shoulder at the man and the woman in the back booth. When I looked they were awfully cuddly. She didn't look like his wife to me.

"Franny Lindeman asked you to marry him, too, didn't he?"

"Yes, he asked me, too. But that was different," she points out sternly, setting down her fork. "Franny Lindeman was always asking me to marry him. He asked me after our very first date, and then kept on asking me over and over again every time we went out."

Before I can ask her 'Well, why did you continue going out with him?' she says, sitting up, "You see, Franny was too short for the army. And pickings were kind of slim during the war. So that's why I kept going out with him, and why I kept saying no."

"Even after he sent you all that money when you were spending the summer with Aunt Lulu in Boston? And isn't it true that you never, not once, wrote back?" I couldn't resist hitting her with these questions, for this was another favorite story of ours: how my mother destroyed a man's life.

Partly because we *saw* this Franny Lindeman one night years ago sitting alone at the ice cream counter in Friendly's on Exeter Road after we'd all gone to see *The Bible* at the Ioka. That time my mother, once she'd spotted her old friend, was embarrassed to death and refused to look at him again, even though his back was to us. Actually, it was my father who recognized him first, since Franny still lives in Exeter, I guess, and is a mailman. Dad claims that when he's in Exeter selling cigarettes he often sees Franny trudging from one house to the other, delivering everyone else's mail. Getting older, paler, shrinking. Looking more and more rejected, my father would, winking at Steve and me, always add.

"Even after he sent me the money," she says. "And yes, I never wrote back. But oh, he didn't send me much! Besides"—over the years she has honed her defense—"if he was foolish enough to send money to an eighteen-year-old girl finally living it up a little with her sister in Boston, and keep on sending it no matter if I ever wrote him or not, didn't I have a right to be foolish enough to spend it?" She always ends this story with that.

She picks up her plastic fork, and we continue to eat.

"So what was it like when you finally met Dad?" It occurs to me as I'm squeezing the last bit of tartar sauce out of its tiny paper cup that we've never gotten this far before. We've always gotten bogged down on Franny Lindeman and whether or not my mother had led him on only to abandon him cruelly; we always talked ourselves out debating that. Though I guess a big part of me felt that she had, it occurs to me now that, although I know generally how the story of my parents' meeting went, I've never heard the specifics.

My mother sets down her fork and sits back. She seems

delighted at what I have asked.

"Well"—she adjusts the glasses on her nose—"when he came home from the war I was boarding at Nana's, like I said, working at the radio station. I knew he was coming home and so I was planning already to move."

I interrupt: "You were in his room?"

"Well, no, I was in Uncle Burt's old room, but it was right next to his and so I was going to move anyway. Would you get me a drink of water?" she asks, motioning to the bubbler in the corner, seeing now that she has my attention and, as seems more and more to be her way, taking advantage of it a bit.

After she's had a drink and has gathered her thoughts, she goes on: "Anyway, Nana was having a big dinner the night he arrived, naturally, to welcome him home. For Aunt Alice and Uncle Burt and Edith and Harry Bath, and Grampa and herself of course—and she wanted me to come too. I didn't want to, it seemed like a family affair, but she wouldn't take no for an answer.

"In fact, when I came home that afternoon from work, before I could get up the front stairs, Nana called me from out in the kitchen. I knew she wanted to introduce me to your father, and frankly I didn't want to meet him. I knew she was prouder than heck that he'd fought in the war, and prouder still that he'd managed to get home in one piece, but *I* really couldn't have cared less. It'd been a long day at work, I guess.

"Well, do you remember that rocking chair she had by the stove? No, you probably wouldn't, but Steve does, I'm sure. Anyway, your father was sitting there in that. Now, Nana had had a picture of him hanging in the hall, so it wasn't the first time I'd seen him—but that picture, well, it wasn't very good or something, because that face was a face only a mother could love. But now, the man sitting in that rocking chair—well, hey, I said to myself. He was tanned and he had nice broad shoulders. He didn't look like he'd just got back from the war, he looked like he'd just got back from Palm Beach! He smiled a lot. He had a good sense of humor, even then, your father. I remember seeing a *lot* of teeth.

"I had dinner with them that night, and the next morning at breakfast your father was up when I got up and offered me a ride to work. I told him I could catch the WBBX station wagon that picked up us workers downtown, but he insisted on giving me a ride. So he drove me to work! And when we got there he asked me if I had a lunch hour. I did. So he met me for lunch! And then he picked me up *after* work and drove me home and asked me if I would like to go to the movies that night. I told him I couldn't. Charlie was leaving for Georgia the next day and had begged me for one more date, as it turned out to see if he couldn't possibly change my mind. 'Tomorrow night?' he asked. And so we went to the movies the very next night."

"What movie?"

"*I* don't know," she laughs. "But when it was over he said, 'Want to take a ride around the beach?' All I could think was that his mother would be furious. Here he just got home after two years away and he was spending all his time with *me!* But we went anyway," she says, and laughs, "and it was somewhere there along Ocean Boulevard—it was pretty dark and deserted then, this was before that part of the beach was built up—he turned to me—he'd die if he knew I was telling you this—and said, 'Are you comfortable way over there? Why don't you move over here a little?' 'No, I'm fine,' I said.

"Well, then I got a little nervous. He'd been off who knows where, in the jungles of Africa or someplace, for *two whole* years. And yet the scariest part was coming up. When we got back into town we were both going to the same exact house! I was scared, I really was. I didn't know if I could trust him or not. But then we got up to the door, and when I was unlocking it, he turned me around and said, 'Would you mind if I kissed you goodnight?' Well, I melted. I wasn't afraid of him any more after that."

She takes her napkin off her lap and folds it in a little square and tucks it under her plate.

There are three things I would like to point out:

1. This doesn't sound like my father at all!

Yesterday afternoon I had to pester him like crazy before he'd go out to the Plains with me to go skating. 'We haven't gone skating in years! It's Sunday!' I said. 'We always used to go skating on Sunday afternoons! I didn't come home 5,000 miles for a visit just to sit around the house!'

He went with me, but he didn't skate very much. When I couldn't spot him out on the ice, I spotted him sitting in the car. 'My ankles,' he said, cracking the window. 'They can't take it any more. *Please.*' He sat there, huddled, his hands between his knees, and seemed happy just to watch.

2. This doesn't even really sound like my mother!

She's sixty one years old. On our way here I had to turn the car around at the federal building because she'd forgotten to put her back bridgework in her mouth. 'No one will notice,' I said. 'I won't go in!' she warned. I looked at her. She was serious, plus they might. We made a U-turn and went home for her teeth.

3. But more importantly, this doesn't sound like THEM!

Before we left home this evening, my mother scribbled a note on the back of an old telephone bill (over which the two of them had probably had a fight) and set it out on the kitchen table for my father—with a plate.

NATE, GONE OUT TO EAT. DINNER IN PAN ON
STOVE. HEAT IT UP.
BACK WHEN WE GET HERE. LOIS.

"Dinner" was American chop suey left over from Friday night, a dish anyone in my family could tell you my father almost hates. And note: not *DEAR NATE,* NATE. Not *LOVE, LOIS,* not *SEE YOU, LOIS,* not *LOIS UNDERLINED,* just plain old LOIS. Could these be the two people she'd just finished telling me about?

She slaps her hand down on the table and says suddenly,

"That's it. I'm going to ask him."

"*Who?*" but I know who. "Don't."

"Sure," she says, taking her lipstick out of her purse and putting on a bit. "Otherwise I won't be able to sleep tonight. I'll always wonder whatever became of poor Charlie Baxter, where he ended up."

"Really," I say, trying to coax her into changing her mind. "You don't really want to bother them, do you? *I'll* tell you about him," I say. "After he left here he met and married a nice Southern girl. They settled down. Bought a house. Had nice kids. He likes his job, he's the vice president of a bank!, but he's thinking about retiring soon. He had a hernia operation last year—"

But already she's gotten up, has taken her glasses off, has put them on the table, where they shine, and is gone.

I can't watch. One of the girls who works here is sitting on a back-up case of Sweetheart paper cups that she's sidled out from under the counter. She has her legs crossed and is mindlessly penning the edge of the white soles of her shoes. The other girl, her partner, is leaning on her elbow on the counter, sipping a Coke through a straw. When she isn't sipping she's playing with the straw, twirling it in her fingers like a tiny baton. Ignoring the two aproned high school boys in paper hats who keep sticking their heads out the pick-up window. Until they leave and then reappear, waving a batch of French fries they've just cooked. *Then* the girls come around.

"Nope," she says, sliding back in, "but it sure did look like him. Spit and image." She drains the water from her cup and sets it upside-down on the table. "Don't worry," she says, "I'm not going to embarrass you. It wasn't him. They've left."

"Franny Lindeman," I say, just as one of the counter girls lets out a sharp laugh. "And now Charlie Baxter. And Dad."

"I told you," she says, tossing her head back and smiling, "if he was foolish enough to mail me that money, I think I had every right to be foolish enough to spend it. And as for

Charlie Baxter, was I supposed to marry him with three days' notice? And where would you be if I had?" She clips the glasses in their quilted case and slips them into her purse. "Humph! I'm sure they're fine," she says. "You know, your father exaggerates about Franny. He was married once, but his poor wife died. You can't blame me for that, though, can you? And Charlie, he's probably *president* of a bank. He's probably a millionaire somewhere," she says. "Humph! He was *smart*."

She looks pretty, actually, now. Without glasses. In lipstick. Lost in thought. I can just barely see it.

"And your father," she says and laughs. "Well, I married him."

We sit here across from one another, silent for a minute.

"Oh, well," she says all of a sudden, as if made antsy by all this talk, looking at the mound of clams still left in her boat. "I guess I'll just ask for a doggie bag. Should I? It'll be a bigger hit than American chop suey! I mean to take the rest of these home in. To your father."

Miss New Hampshire and the Watermelon Thief

IN 1978, his sister was Miss New Hampshire. Across the table, his niece is looking through a scrapbook loaded with pictures from that year:

There's his sister in her banner and crown, flat on her back, giving a pint of blood at a Red Cross drawing.

There's his sister in the middle of a lineup of shovel-wielding state officials breaking ground for the Fox Run Mall.

There's his sister pumping the first gallon of gas at the gala opening of Dover Point's first self-serve filling station.

"You know, Shelley," his sister, sitting next to him says, "your Uncle Billy put that together."

"Did you?" Shelley asks.

But she catches him with his mouth full of muffin—and then the buzzer sounds.

His sister is drawing on her just-lit cigarette. She holds in the smoke and rolls her eyes. She peeks through the curtains and tosses the matches onto the table and tucks the cigarette into the nub in the ashtray. "Be right back," she says, exhaling, then she slips out the kitchen door and heads toward the garage which she and her husband converted into a produce stand in order to supplement his income as a grade school principal by selling the vegetables they grow out back.

He can hear his sister talking to the customer—"Oh she's fine, for now," he can hear her say—while Shelley lifts her hand from the lap of her bathrobe and rolls back a thick black page.

There's his sister in Loudon on a grandstand handing out four-foot-tall trophies at the annual motorbike races.

There's his sister posed between an incredibly fat couple as if ready to cut the ribbon at their new laundromat with a giant pair of cardboard scissors.

There's his sister behind the knobbed helm of the *Mt. Washington* (here her crown is replaced by a braided captain's cap) on Lake Winnipesaukee on the Fourth of July.

Also:

There's his sister sitting on committees.

His sister dining at head tables.

His sister riding in parades from Colebrook to Rye Beach, perched on fire trucks or the backs of convertibles or on elaborate papier-mâché floats.

In all of the pictures, his sister is the center of attention. She's always smiling. Always poised.

Though it's true he put it together, he hasn't set eyes on it—the scrapbook—in ages. In fact, he's all but forgotten how many of these appearances his sister made. Not to mention what a knockout she was. And she was what, then? Barely eighteen.

"Uncle Billy?"

"Yes, Shelley?" he says.

"Uncle Billy, who took these?"

The book lies open to a page of photos of his sister in Derry, New Hampshire, with Alan Shepard on *Alan Shepard Day*.

"I did," he says upon looking. He slides the album back in front of her. "Your grandmother and I followed your mother all over the state that year. Wherever she went, we went, just about!"

"He was the first man in space," Shelley says, and then for the first time since he arrived an hour earlier she turns her attention away from the scrapbook to one of the giant blueberry muffins he picked up at the Muffinry on the short drive across town. She peels back the fluted paper. "How old *are* you anyway, Uncle Billy?" she asks.

"How old am I?" he laughs. "Twenty-six."

"So, how old would that make you back then?"

"Oh," he says when he sees where she's headed. "Well, 1978. That was the year I turned thirteen. Look at this one!" he says, pointing to a clipping of his sister standing on a platform decorated with huge scallops of bunting. She's with the man who was the governor at that time, and her arm is plunged to the shoulder in a wheel-sized, wire basket. "That's when your mother drew the winning lottery number. Hey doesn't that man who won still stop in to buy produce? Your mother told me he was for a while. When he'd heard she'd gone into business. He lives in a big house in Rye now, evidently. He drives a fancy car. I guess he felt it was the least he could do!"

Shelley shrugs. She's only just turned eight, yet—besides her thinning hair, and her terrible gauntness, and her pale, pale skin—a gauze patch covers one eye whose use she's lost already. "That's funny," she says.

What's funny? he thinks. That he didn't have anything better to do that year than drag his mother to all of his sister's personal appearances? Because, yes, that is what he did. *He* was the one—at first, at least—who was most eager to follow along.

But Shelley's attention is still on the clipping. "They use ping-pong balls with numbers on them now, you know."

"You're right, they do!" he says, and then they sit there quietly, looking through the scrapbook together, until his sister, having cashed out her customer, comes back inside.

"So, Billy, can you *believe* it?" she says, shucking the old coat she's had on all morning. She reaches between them and retrieves her cigarette. "Can you?" she says, "*I* can't!"

The night before when his mother picked him up at the airport, one of the first things she said when they got in her car was that his sister had something she was dying to tell him.

"What?" he asked anxiously. "Is it news about Shelley?"

"Oh, no. You mean a remission? No, Billy, I'm sorry, it's not that."

"Well, what then? You can't bring it up and not tell me," he warned.

"But I'm not supposed to, Billy. I can't."

It didn't take long, though, before his mother gave in. "Oh, *all right*," she said, "but you've got to promise me you won't tell her I told you."

He promised, and then, as they whizzed down the highway, resignedly she spilled the beans:

"Do you remember the man who gypped you out of the price of one of your sister's watermelons when you came home to visit last summer and covered at the stand when they first took Shelley in to the specialist in Boston?" she waited for a show of recognition. "Well," she said, "he came back."

"He came back?"

"Yes. He came back."

"Is that what she's been dying to tell me?"

His mother nodded her head. "He came back, and he gave Jack the same line of baloney he gave you evidently and gypped him out of the price of a watermelon, too. Yes, ha-ha, I know," she said, "but your sister has been nearly sick over it, let me tell you. In fact, so sick, I'm worried," she said. "It doesn't sound like her, I know, but it's true! It's all she's talked about for the last three days! 'Wait till I tell Billy,' she keeps saying. She also says she's sure she warned Jack about him, but poor Jack swears she didn't."

He pooh-poohed his mother's concern, but sure enough, when he had borrowed her car come morning and pulled into his sister's driveway, his sister came right out to greet him and immediately began to tell him what had happened.

And now, though she has already been over it all once, she seems gung-ho to start in again.

"Can you *believe* the nerve of some people?" she says. "I wanted to call the police, but Jack wouldn't let me. He kept saying it was only seven dollars! *Times two*, I had to remind him, *times two!* But it's the principle of the thing, anyway, don't you think?" She blows the smoke over her shoulder so that it won't bother Shelley, and then she breaks one of the giant muffins in two and puts half of it on the plate in front of her. "He had Massachusetts plates. He drove a big, bluish-gray car. You said it was an Impala or something, right?"

"I think so," he says, not sure. He remembers the incident certainly, but not nearly as well as she. "It was something big," he says, while his sister looks at him, eager, all ears. "It's just—well, are you sure you didn't sell a whole watermelon to this man who spoke to Jack?"

"Oh, Billy," she says, disappointed, "I haven't sold a whole watermelon yet this summer. I know it sounds crazy to think that anyone would be foolish enough to try that trick at the same place twice, but I'm sure it was him. I'm sure of it," she says, and takes another drag from her cigarette, and, this time, blows the smoke straight up. "He must have just remembered who waited on him before and recognized it wasn't Jack. He had his wife with him," she says, as if poking at his memory. "He left her in the car."

Did *he* tell her this? he wonders. "Did I—"

"No, Jack did," she says.

He looks at Shelley sitting between them, still scouring through the book, and though he would like to, really wants to, he just can't remember if the man who hoodwinked him left his wife sitting in the car. All he can remember are a few very hazy details: that the man himself was sixty-ish, he thinks, and wore one of those leisure shirts with embroidery down the front that always reminded him on sight of barbers.

"He told Jack the same thing he told you," she goes on. "He said he stopped by and bought a watermelon a few days ago and that when he got it home and cut it open discovered the thing had gone bad."

There *is* one other detail he remembers, however. "Did he say he bought it for a party?"

"Yes! I told you it was him! He said he bought it for a party and that he had to throw the whole thing out! Ingenious, isn't it?" She shakes her head. "The whole cockamamie story was designed to make *us* feel guilty for leaving *him* dessert-less with his friends!" She clucks her tongue. She can hardly sit still—

All this while Shelley, having looked up from the scrapbook, waits patiently for a place to jump in.

"Can you be*lieve* it?" she says. "God, what a racket!" She twists her cigarette deep into the ashtray. "He probably drives around all day and hits every little produce stand he comes across—at seven dollars or whatever a whack! When I came in from grocery shopping and Jack asked me if I'd sold a whole watermelon a few days ago, I knew right then it was him!"

"Excuse me. Mom? *Mom?*"

But his sister doesn't hear.

"'Why?' I asked him. And when he told me, Billy, my heart sank. I made him sit right down right then and tell me *exactly* what the man had said. Oh, Billy," she says, slumped in her chair, pushing up her sleeves, "why couldn't he have come while *I* was here? I'd give anything to have been the one to have waited on him! I'd have recognized that stupid story! I'd—I'd have given him a piece of my mind!!"

"*Mom?*"

"*What?*" she snaps, so that Shelley, frightened, shrinks back; and then all three of them sit there, shaken. Until his sister gets a grip on herself.

"Shel—oh sweetie, I'm sorry," she says. "Mommy isn't angry at you. Did you think Mommy was angry at you?" She pushes the ashtray into the middle of the table and leans forward and speaks softly to the little girl. "What is it, hon?" she asks, stroking the hair from Shelley's forehead. "Hm, Shel? Just tell me. What?"

Shelley swallows, and, after a few more assurances, is finally coaxed into revealing her question. "Who was it you said won? Miss Texas?"

"What, sweetie? Oh yes." His sister laughs a little, startled. "That's right. Miss Texas won."

By now Shelley is at the back of the book, to the pictures of the Miss America Pageant in Atlantic City. And it's these pictures, as he looks over at them now, that remind him of something else he has also almost forgotten: the sudden, unprepared-for turn in events that ended that tumultuous year.

First, there's his sister in the lobby of the oceanfront hotel that was the official Miss America Headquarters signing her name in the minuscule space that was New Hampshire on their gigantic U.S. map.

Then there's his sister squeezed between the shoulder blades of the other New England states during a drummed-up, windy, crack-of-dawn photo session on the boardwalk on one of those old-fashioned trollies.

And then, when Shelley flips the page, there's his sister as a pale pink speck on the runway in Independence Hall during her preliminary bathing suit competition.

As a blue speck on the next night in evening gown.

And as a kind of silvery speck on the third night in a beaded cocktail dress, holding a mike up in front of her face, singing—for, though no one could really hear her from the fourth balcony where he and his mother sat, singing was his sister's "talent."

It's really no surprise, though, he thinks as he looks at these final pictures, that not one of them has been glued to the book's heavy pages. As if signaling an abrupt end to his interest that year, they've only been stuck in between.

The very last that Shelley removes is of his sister in the

cavernous front lobby with her official chaperone—whom she shared with Nevada and New Jersey—between a series of hectic rehearsals before that final, televised night.

After this, well, the pictures ran out.

You see, in spite of the flashy wardrobe bought with money his mother had to borrow, and in spite of the last-minute voice lessons to which they drove his sister up to Manchester twice a week, and in spite of the endless kitchen-table conferences with a friend of a friend who sold Avon on the most becoming hairstyle and makeup, naturally his sister didn't win. In front of everyone in town who stayed up, she didn't even make the Top Ten.

What they didn't realize until much too late, of course, was that she never had a chance. Not against those huge states like Ohio and Texas who ran their pageants and pushed their contestants with all the gusto of big business. But, carried away, they had thought that she did. Buoyed by the ease with which she had taken the local and state pageants, they had somehow managed to convince themselves that fame and wealth were hers. Hers was theirs as well, of course, and so they were startled and deeply disappointed to find the whole thing was over so quick.

In fact, he remembers that when they got back home he and his mother—his father had already been dead then for years—spent close to a week sitting in a daze at the kitchen table. Among flowers and telegrams from friends (NICE TRY! BOY, YOU LOOKED GREAT! OBVIOUSLY THOSE JUDGES WOULDN'T KNOW A WINNER OF THEY TRIPPED OVER ONE!), which were clearly meant for his sister but which were confiscated, in a way, by them, they moped and sipped cold tea. They were perfectly, selfishly helpless, he remembers, so that even his mother's cousin Agnes who lived a forty-five minute drive upstate felt it necessary to borrow a car from a neighbor, drive down, and cook them their meals, to make sure they were eating at least.

In short, this was not what he would ever call one of his

family's shining moments. And *that's* why he supposes he had blocked it all out. Oh, they got over the disappointment soon enough, but then they were embarrassed and, frankly ashamed that they had ever let it count for so much.

But of course Shelley is oblivious to all of this. She simply flops the stack of pages back in one clump and starts flipping through again.

"Shel, sweetie, for goshsakes," his sister says, "don't you want your muffin?"

Shelley looks at it and picks it up and takes a nibble, and for a minute—a second, really—as his sister watches Shelley chew, one hand holding her bandage in place, her face goes completely blank.

She recovers quickly, though, and tosses her head toward the scrapbook. She says, "Boy, we were young then, weren't we? I thought I'd lost that thing a long time ago, but then last week I was going through some of my old school things at mother's and *voila*—there it was! I threw all the trophies out, and that godawful crown, but for old-times' sake *it* seemed worth saving."

He wants to apologize for the way he acted those many years ago, but before he can, she is asking how work is going, and how he likes his new place.

He teaches math at a prep school in San Francisco, and for about a month he has lived in a house-share in that city's Sunset District. He tells his sister about both of these ventures, and then he tells her about his plans to rent a cabin with friends for a week in Tahoe next winter. This reminds her to ask about his trip to Hawaii and to thank him for the postcard he sent.

Still, through all of this casual back-and-forth, he can tell that the crazy watermelon incident hasn't really left her mind. In fact, she can't help but bring it up occasionally, (only quietly now, in deference to Shelley) in order to say something about it, like how unfair the whole thing seems.

It's after one of these calmer outbursts that suddenly his

sister says, "You know what our problem is as I see it, Billy? We're all of us just too nice." She's pouring Shelley a glass of milk. Refolding the spout and returning the carton to the fridge, she says, "I mean, Billy, just think about it, will you? Jack even admitted he thought there was something evil about that guy, but then he went ahead and apologized anyway and *insisted* on returning his money!"

After this, the buzzer sounds again, and, when his sister has gone back outside, he tries to remember how *she* reacted to the disappointment of Atlantic City.

For two days, he remembers, after they got back home, his sister didn't even get dressed. She just lay in her bed in her room upstairs all day, with the radio on her nightstand on low and her face turned toward the wall. She ignored Cousin Agnes' meals. For two days she left her hair up until it fell to her shoulders, her eyes dark with makeup until the stuff rubbed off. But she never cried or complained or said much of anything as he remembers, though it's true he was so preoccupied with his own disappointment that she might have and he just didn't notice.

But on the third day—aha! he remembers—*she* got up before everyone else. She showered and dressed and, wearing her hair the simple way she had always worn it, was at the table eating a stack of Cousin Agnes' French toast when he and his mother padded down. They hardly touched the spread that was laid out that morning, but his sister—she ate and ate. And then she gathered up her books, as if nothing had ever happened, and off she went to school. She was still a senior at Clipper High, head cheerleader, Pep Club president. It was his sister, he remembers, relieved, who led the way during that particular family crisis toward resuming their normal lives.

She'd made it that time, but would she this?

It's been a year since that last visit home, and Shelley's condition has gotten much worse. In February she lost her sight completely, and shortly after that she was confined to her bed. But it wasn't until this May just past that his mother, with whom he speaks at least once every week, reported that his sister had finally consented to admitting Shelley to a facility in Boston which could provide her with the necessary round-the-clock care.

Through all of this his mother's reports were primarily reports on Shelley, but more recently they've been reports on his sister and the toll this is taking on her.

"She won't admit it, of course," his mother said recently, "but both she and Jack are exhausted. They get up at the crack of dawn every morning, work at the stand or out in the garden or at school all day, and then drive into Boston—right at rush hour!—every night. Oh, Billy, it's so sad," she said, "but it's all just a matter of time. I hate to say it, but it's true," she said. "It's all just a matter of time."

That's a refrain he's still not used to, though when the phone rings just after six one Saturday morning, waking his entire house, he uses the short time it takes him to stumble to the extension downstairs to brace himself for the worst.

He always imagined it would be his mother who would make the call, but the voice on the line isn't hers.

"Billy?" his sister says. "Billy, guess what! You won't believe this! I caught him!"

"You caught him? Who?" He's puzzled.

"*Him,*" she says. "The watermelon thief! Just yesterday. About four o'clock. I finally got my chance! When the buzzer buzzed and I looked out the window and saw that blue car with the Massachusetts plates—and his wife sitting there in it, just like Jack said—I couldn't believe it. I think my heart stopped beating."

She tells him in detail how she went outside, shaking, and forced herself to play along while he repeated the same old stupid story about buying a watermelon for a party he was having and cutting into it later at home only to find it smelled awful inside.

"And when he was finished," she says, "I said, 'Would you mind waiting here just a minute? The person who you say sold it to you, that must have been my husband. Let me call him, he's out back in our garden.' Billy, Jack wasn't even home yet," she cries, "but that made the guy turn white! 'Oh, that's not necessary,' he said. 'There's no problem really. I just thought you might want to know.' 'Of course there's a problem!' I said, and then, Billy, I wish you could have been here. I ripped up one side of that man and ripped down the other. Of course, he denied everything, but I still grabbed a paper bag and a magic marker and made a big show of taking down his license plate number—in giant black letters!

"Billy? Billy, are you there?—"

"Yes, I'm here," he says.

"Shoot, I thought I'd lost you! Well, anyway, then Jack—thank God!—drove in, and then the guy was sunk. Jack recognized him immediately, of course. You should have heard him sputter then! He didn't know what to say! 'There's been some mistake,' he said. 'Are you *kidding?*' I said, and then he headed for his car. I followed him but went over to his wife's side and knocked on her window instead. He'd left the motor running, with the air conditioning on, no less. 'Do you realize what your husband has been doing?' I yelled. To tell you the truth, Billy, I don't think that she did. She was crocheting squares for an Afghan or something. He probably told her he was just stopping to check the place out, see what we were selling this year. Anyway, she looked at me over the tops of her glasses—then at him—then back at me. 'He's a *thief,*' I yelled, 'the worst kind! He steals from decent, hardworking people. From people with enough things to worry about without having to worry about the likes of him!' Then I couldn't stop myself, Billy, I yelled 'Our little girl—she has cancer, you know! We have medical bills you couldn't even imagine! Do you really think—do you really *really* think we can afford *his* stupid games?' She was just sitting there with her mouth wide open. I could tell that she was just about to roll down her window, but by then he had the car in drive. I don't care though, Billy. I got my wish. They spun out and that was it."

"Well," he says, his voice still froggy, but his heart now pounding less. "Well, that's really—great."

"It is, isn't it?" she says. "I suppose I should feel sorry for his wife. But I don't," she says. "I don't."

"What—why?" he says.

"No, I don't," she says, "I really don't." Then:

"Do you want to say hi to Jack?"

"How about that!" his brother-in-law says. "I tell you, Bill, when your sister was through with that guy he sure left here in a hurry! I doubt we'll ever see him again!"

And after he told his version of what happened, his sister comes back on.

"So, when are we going to see you again?" she asks. "You know, it's been nearly a year."

He tells her that he hopes to be home again soon—perhaps as early as the end of next month. He doesn't say that that is unless, of course, there's any reason to come home sooner.

"Well, I just had to tell you the good news!" she says.

They talk a little more—about the weather on each of the coasts, and about the garden and the peas that are just coming in, and then he forces himself to dampen the mood. "So, how's Shelley?" he asks.

There's a pause, after which his sister says, "Oh things are the same, I guess. But we haven't given up hope. How can we? Of course, the doctors, they aren't very hopeful. But really, Billy, how can we?"

Fancy Cars and Their Owners

FOR THE FIRST TIME in years there she is. On television. The local news. Maurice Harris is doing part two of his feature on fancy cars and their owners.

Hey look, I say, *what's-her-name!*

My mother puts the paper in her lap.

The kitchen table creaks as my father leans over so he can see into the den. (He just got home from work. He's still eating the tuna casserole my mother cooked him for dinner.)

Maurice asks her if she'll give him a tour of the inside. It's a black and silver Mustang, souped-up, parked in the middle of somebody's front lawn. The television camera keeps shooting it from different angles. The sun's catching all over it. The front fender, the side-view mirrors, the chrome door handles. So the whole screen's flashing like distant warfare.

Isn't that her? I say. Yes. That's her.

Well, this is my speedometer, she says. And this is my clock. This is my CB—my handle? Black Knight—and this is my shift. She pushes the clutch in and runs down the gears. This is my ash tray. My air conditioning vents. My lighter. She takes it out, shows him the coil, pops it back in. (She's sitting in the driver's seat. The camera's taking a shot over her shoulder. I see right off that her fingertips are still yellow from smoking.) This is my tape deck. My odometer. Those are my emergency flashers. That's about it, I guess. I've got solid-state speakers in the back.

I look at my mother who makes a face as if to say, Well,

what do you know, there she is.

She's one of the kids from the South End I grew up with. It takes me a while, though to remember her right name. Pamela? I think. No. Patricia?

I spend eight hours a day driving around in it, she says. I do all the maintenance myself. Everything. Change the oil. Give it a lube job when it needs it. I just put new spark plugs in yesterday morning. I spend about two hours a day keeping it up.

Not Patricia, Priscilla! That's it: Priscilla.

She looks exactly the same as the last time I saw her, whenever that was. Very tall, and she still has long, thin hair. Still so thin that I remember all at once how her ears used to suddenly poke out.

Still homelier than a hedge fence, my father says to us from the kitchen.

Remember her? I yell back to him when I realize he's watching.

I remember playing hide-and-seek after dinner over at the Haven School. Her sitting there on the steps in front of the school doors smoking. The doors were our goals. She was always smoking. Grinding cigarette after cigarette under her sneaker. Pulling one out after another, lighting it up. We thought of her all the time as a grown-up. None of us knew exactly where she lived. She never played hide-and-seek. She was too old for hide-and-seek. She just sat there, leaning casually to one side whenever one of us dashed past her for the goals. Her cigarettes set in her lap. Her elbow propped on her knee. Blowing smoke in long tusks out her nose.

My mother says, Huh. What *was* her name?

Priscilla *what*? I think to myself.

There's a shot of her driving to work. Driving out. Pulling into a filling station, looking under the hood with the attendant. (They must've followed her all day with their minicam.) A shot of her throwing a dime into a basket at a toll. Stopping at a Minit Mart for groceries. Dropping her bags in the trunk, whumping it shut. She has on a purple windbreaker with lettering on the back that says GRANITE STATE AUTO CLUB. Her thin hair hops off her shoulders when she ducks in. While she's digging for the safety belt, it spreads across her back like a deck of cards strung carefully across a table top. Until she finds it and sits up. Pulls the buckle-side around.

Now she's back on the front lawn and she's saying, I clear two hundred dollars a week at my job at Simplex and I spend oh, about fifty of it each week on gas. I belong to a hot rod club in Nashua. I've made a whole lot of friends there. I make a lot of friends too just out on the street. Boys pull right up along side me when I stop at stoplights. They even leave me notes under the windshield wipers!

She laughs, bends her head, looks up. Here comes a blush.

She had the first banana bicycle in the neighborhood. I remember the day she appeared with it on the playground. Fixed up with all those goo-ga's we would've killed one another for. A sissy-bar with a jumbo reflector. A zebra-striped seat cover. A front light and back light that worked on the same generator. A horn. Streamers!

No one knew she could even ride a bicycle, then there she was, on the handsomest bike we'd ever seen. Hide-and-seek went right out the window. She lapped around the Haven School playground switching gears, picking up speed, zipping in-and-out between the basketball backboards. Popping wheelies—turned out she could wheely farther than anyone we knew—squiggling fast as the eye between the monkey bars. Just watching was enough to make you dizzy. When she got going she pulled her legs up, she put her sneakers against the handgrips and steered with her feet. She didn't even brake the normal way. She stood up, pumped a few good ones, then skidded sideways. Looking back over her shoulder as she hopped off to see how much rubber she'd laid.

She let anyone ride it who wanted to. There's only one rule, she said. No going outside the playground.

No one else ever looked very good, after her.

She tells Maurice how one time someone wrote I love you on the hood with a Magic Marker. She had a heck of a time getting if off. She used about four different kinds of waxes, she says. She tells him about the time the Volvo drove into her. She saw it coming, but there was another car behind her. She couldn't do anything but sit there and watch. I cried my eyes out in the back of the cruiser, she says, smiling, rolling her head back, blushing a second time.

While we fight heatedly with one another over her bicycle (*I hosied it next.* LIAR! *I did!*) she swings up onto the top of the monkey bars, shakes out a cigarette and lights it and draws on it and flicks it against the bar she's sitting on so the ashes trail down to the pavement. She puts the pack back into her pocket and rolls the lit end against the bar, making a point. Until she's ready to draw on it again. Her eyes half-closed. She blows the smoke straight up into the air.

She was only in the sixth-grade, but boy, she sure knew how to smoke a cigarette.

Why do you do it, Maurice says, spend all that time, all that money? He puts the microphone up to her face and she says:

Well. One day I said so what if I have big teeth, they're my own. So what if my ears are big, I can hear, can't I? Everybody ought to have something. For me, it's my car.

While Maurice is signing off she opens the door and gets in. Sure enough her hair falls forward, her ears all of a sudden poke out.

I say, Her last name started with an L, I think. Laycock?

Carefully she backs it off the lawn.

I wonder where that is? my mother says.

It looks like Elwynn Park to me. (My father from the kitchen with his mouth full.)

And then the camera switches from Maurice to Priscilla, just as she's shifting into forward, pulling off down the street—How could she afford something like that working at

Simplex? my father says—and zooms in up close as she picks up speed, then settles back a little as the chrome-spoked hubcaps begin to sparkle and blur, and look like they're rolling backward.

Priscilla *Lackey*, I remember all at once.

Right. That's it, my mother says, snapping the paper. I wonder what ever happened to that girl.

The Note

MR. KELLEY is out in his driveway washing his car. He's had a lot of free time on his hands lately. He retired from his job on the navy yard last Spring.

He gets up at six every morning and reads the newspaper cover-to-cover. With a cup of coffee and a bowl of instant cereal. And then he puts his shoes on and washes his dishes and sets them on the counter to dry. He goes out in the yard and potters around.

Mr. Kelley is out in his driveway washing his car when—

He paints whatever needs painting. (Whatever's been splintered by the dank salt air.) He rakes leaves. He prunes the crabapple trees. Cuts back the grape vines. Mows the lawn. He thins the hedge of forsythia bushes down back.

In the afternoon? Well, sometimes he goes to the town library then. He browses through the books they have on trains. There are a surprising number of books on trains in the town library, and trains are his hobby, if he has one.

Mr. Kelley is out in his driveway washing his car when a woman in one of the new apartments across the street—

He's amazed, you might say, by the technology. How anyone could ever have built a railroad from one coast to the other is beyond him. And to think, they first did it over a hundred years ago! Just from Boston to Poland Spring was a miracle. He remembers, of course, when they ran regularly through the town. When there were club cars, dining cars, sleepers. When train travel was posh and the norm. When an *automobile* was a luxury very few could afford.

Or sometimes in the afternoon he goes out to his daughter's. He stays for coffee and listens while his daughter's mother-in-law, who has a room up over his daughter's garage, chews his ear off about her ills. High blood pressure, a bum back, water retention in her legs. His daughter is between them folding laundry on her kitchen table. The mother-in-law, tapping her matches on an ashtray, is squinting, talking, a cigarette bobbing in her mouth. She says, "those are the troubles I guess you're stuck with when you're fat."

Mr. Kelley, however, is tall and thin. His friends on the yard called him SLIM.

(Or sometimes in the afternoon he goes food shopping. Or visits old family friends, neighbors and such, from when he grew up on the other side of town.)

Mr. Kelley is out in his driveway washing his car when a woman in one of the new apartments across the street runs out onto her patio in her nightgown—

At night he watches television. Television! Talk about technology!

When a woman in one of the new apartments across the street runs out onto her patio in her nightgown and—

He does most all the cooking. His wife is still around—*boy is she*, he would put it, *and if you don't believe me, I've got the phone bills to prove it!*—but doing the cooking and the cleaning—it's all right. He's got lots of free time on his hands!

Too *much* time, some might say.

Watch out you don't go off your rocker! his friends on the navy yard said.

He scrubs floors. He vacuums. He dusts.

Mr. Kelley is out in his driveway washing his car when a woman in one of the new apartments across the street runs out onto her patio in her nightgown and hollers.

The gin bottle seems to hover in the air, then smashes not far from his feet.

And then a man suddenly appears and grabs ahold of the woman and drags her back inside. From the way they paw at one another, stumbling, it's clear that they're drunk. The drapes draw shut in three slashes.

Mr. Kelley carefully sets the hose on the lawn and walks down the driveway and picks up the note. He has trouble reading it.

> PLEASE HELP ME MY HUSBAND HAS GONE WEST. CALL MY BROTHER-IN-LAW PLEASE 430-6372 AND TELL HIM TO COME TO MARY'S RIGHT AWAY. MY HUSBAND HAS TRIPPED ON THE PHONE. *PLEASE.* I'M AFRAID OF WHAT HE MIGHT DO NEXT!

He turns the water off and goes into the house and gets his glasses from the top of the refrigerator. He struggles to make better sense out of the print. Finally he's figured it out.

> PLEASE HELP ME MY HUSBAND HAS GONE *WILD.* CALL MY BROTHER-IN-LAW PLEASE 430-6372 AND TELL HIM TO COME TO MARY'S RIGHT AWAY. MY HUSBAND HAS *RIPPED OUT* THE PHONE. *PLEASE.* I'M AFRAID OF WHAT HE MIGHT DO NEXT!

Mr. Kelley goes into the den and pulls the footstool up to the TV tray where the Kelleys keep their phone.

He puts his head in his hands for a minute, and then he sits up and braces himself and dials the number, still not sure what he's going to say. *Your brother is abusing his wife?... Your sister-in-law needs you??* This last might be the best thing, then hang up. No sense to getting involved, he thinks, when Mrs. Kelley, with pillow creases still fresh on her cheek (the tea-kettle clock on the kitchen wall says eight-twenty), with her hair pressed flat on one side, plods down the stairs and enters the den.

"Who are you calling?" she asks, her voice cracked with sleep.

Mr. Kelley hangs up. No one answered.

"*Who are you calling?*" she asks, again.

He hands her the note and rubs his hands together. He explains to her what happened.

Mrs. Kelley opens her old bathrobe and rewraps it tighter around her. She cinches the belt so that it almost cuts her in half. "What did I tell you? Didn't I tell you?" she says. "I knew those apartments spelled trouble."

She sits down in the La-Z-Boy and crosses her ankles. Reclines back so that her belly, with the note sitting on top, rises slowly, fully, like a cake. "Didn't I tell you those apartments spelled trouble?" she says, then yawns and closes her eyes.

Mr. Kelley plucks the note from her stomach.

He lets it ring longer this time, but still no one answers.

He hangs up and after sitting there and just thinking for a minute goes into the living room and leans over the couch that's beneath the large window in the front of the house. He looks out across the lawn past the Kelley's flower beds to the apartment patio where the drapes are still shut tight. While he's looking, something suddenly bumps against them—bumps just once, but hard. "Christ. Her brother-in-law's not home," he calls back over his shoulder. "Jesus Christ. What do you think we should do?"

Mrs. Kelley opens her eyes.

"Her brother-in-law. He's not home. *What should we do?*" he repeats.

"'We'?" Mrs. Kelley says, "*You.* I didn't pick up that note." She drops her head back against the chair.

"But she may be in trouble," he says.

"Who?"

"The *woman*," he says.

Mrs. Kelley sits up and pushes herself to her feet. She sighs reluctantly. She clears her throat.

"Was she skinny? A little knock-kneed? Did she have bright yellow hair? Because if she did she used to be married to what's-her-face's brother. Shirley Reese. She used to be married to her brother," she says. "They're separated now, of course—she and Shirley Reese's brother. Know why? Drank like a fish."

She crosses the den and enters the living room. "I thought I saw her going into those damn apartments the other day. That woman, I said to myself, that woman looks like Mary LaVallee. The drapes still drawn?" she asks, dropping her bulk in a big whoosh on the couch.

"Yes," Mr. Kelley says.

"Her whole family's a bunch of tough ones, the LaVallees. She and her brothers and sisters terrorized us kids in Maple Haven growing up. Always they hogged the tetherball courts. Every single one of them smoked by the time they were ten. The girls wore makeup to grade school! I wouldn't worry," she says. "She just ran out and hollered and then flung the bottle?"

"*Yes*," he says, still not moving his eyes from the patio.

"I wouldn't worry," she says. "Don't waste your time. Those LaVallees can take care of themselves. But her brother-in-law. Now I wonder who that would be? I wonder who she's married to now? I don't remember any announcement in the paper. Do you?"

Mrs. Kelley puts her thinking cap on—"I bet Helen would know," she says, "but it's a little early to call her right now"—while Mr. Kelley goes back into the den and redials the phone. When he returns, "No one answers?"

"No," he says.

"She just ran out and hollered and flung the bottle?"

"*YES*," Mr. Kelley says.

"All right, all right. Don't get nasty," she says. She gets up off the couch and goes over to the bay window and looks out at the foot of the driveway, at the shards of broken glass. "Hmm," Mrs. Kelley says. She leans on the window sill and looks at the car which is beginning to steam as the sun clears the Cook's house next door. "Hmm," she says again. She goes over to the rocker and sits down in it and puts her hands into her bathrobe pockets. She pulls out two gold-loop earrings. "*Hmm*," she says—she hadn't expected to find them there—and tipping her head, first one way then the other, squinting, she clips them on.

~

He had thought to himself when the sunlight woke him up, these days one day is just like the rest. What can I do to make today a little different?

He had thought and had settled for washing the car.

He had driven down to Tibbet's and bought a four-dollar can of turtle wax. An extravagance for Mr. Kelley (he's on a pension), but he had thought while he was at it he might as well go all out.

Their entire street—both ways—was deserted. He was whistling, rinsing the hood, when the woman across the street ran out. He thinks now that before she hollered she must have waved to get his attention. ("*My husband has ripped out the phone!*") He thinks now that there may very well have been blood in what he glimpsed of her husband's cold eyes.

"It must be that older fellow from Dover they said she was going out with," she says. "You know. The ex-plumber," she says. "The one who came here a couple of years ago to fix the washer. Remember? It was on the fritz again just after he left. *That's* who she must have married," she says. "In fact, Helen told me she saw them together. And that he bends the elbow, too."

"I'm going to call the police," he says.

"The police?" Mrs. Kelley sits up. "Oh don't call the *police*," she pleads.

"Yes," he says. "I'm going to. Right now."

But he waits almost half an hour before he does. He props his glasses up on his head. He paces the room. He throws out a stack of newspapers and magazines next to her chair in the den. He tidies the hutch, cleans up the mess she made cracking peanuts last night.

"All right, call. Call!" she says when she can't take his fussing about any longer. "But for God's sake, don't give them your name. That's all we need, those LaVallees, all grown up, after *us*."

"Has the paper come yet?" she asks.

He goes out into the driveway and finishes rinsing the car. He pours the soapy water that's left in the bucket into the drywell. He winds up the hose and hangs it from a hook in the garage. He puts the turtle wax on the shelf, unopened. Gathers the buckets and sponges. Carries them around to the shed in the back of the house. He does all of this as quickly as possible, so as to be out of sight by the time they arrive.

He fills the tea kettle at the kitchen sink and puts it on the burner.

Mrs. Kelley decides, upon scuffing into the kitchen, that she would like some coffee, too, please.

She sits down at the kitchen table. "I knew that as soon as those new apartments were finished the neighborhood would go ka-*put*, straight to hell. Didn't I know it? Didn't I say that?" she says.

When the tea kettle whistles, Mr. Kelley grabs it from the burner as if shushing it. He pours for the both of them and carries their cups to the table. He goes back to the refrigerator and gets her the milk.

They sit there. They drink their coffee.

"*Ouch!* That's *hot*," she says. "What? Didn't you cool mine with an ice cube?" she snaps.

"Sorry," he says. "I forgot."

He gets up again to get her some ice.

From their kitchen window the sunlight in their back yard is brilliant. The birds in the birdhouses he built are all chirping like mad.

She tests the temperature of her coffee with her finger. "Nice out, huh?" she says.

Without answering, Mr. Kelley sets his cup in its saucer and gets up and goes into the living room, to the front window.

Two cruisers, lights flashing, are at the curb. Four policemen are rallying. One speaks into his radio. They go inside.

A minute later, the patio door whips open and the woman, still in her nightgown, runs out. She scooches down and grabs ahold of the rail. It takes all the strength two policemen can muster to free her hands and wrestle them behind her in order to clamp on the cuffs.

Then, their black caps askew, the artillery hanging from their belts bumping wildly against their legs, they hustle her back inside through the sliders, and shortly afterwards, out the apartment's front door.

The two other policemen, escorting the man—arms flailing—soon follow. In age and dress, though disheveled, Mr. Kelley notes, the man looks much like himself.

There's a small group now gathered in front. The Dy-Dee diaper man and Ben Watson, the town's water meter reader. And some of the local kids, still sleepy-eyed, straddling their bikes. Also Mr. Cook, who's still in his pajamas. And Mr. Franzen with Chester, his beagle, on his leash, pulling, yelping.

While the four policemen, who are still struggling to keep the couple apart, are conferring back and forth on what they might possibly do next, the woman spits at the man, who ducks, then reels up. Straining from their hold, he spits back.

"They'll see you if you keep looking out the window like that," Mrs. Kelley says soberly from the kitchen.

"No they won't," Mr. Kelley says, stepping back. "They can't see me," he says. "No one's looking over here, anyway." Then under his breath so that you can hardly hear it, "No one, thanks to you, you old witch."

The tea kettle clock on the wall says nine-fifteen when

Mr. Kelley leaves the window and comes back into the kitchen and opens the cupboard. It's still early, but he needs something to do.

Mrs. Kelley sips from her cup. "Keep your nose out of other people's bee's-wax. If I've learned anything in my lifetime, I've learned that."

"What are you going to want for lunch? Tuna fish?" he asks. Noticing a bottle of cooking sherry on the cupboard's top shelf and wondering how the stuff would taste straight.

"Tuna's all right," Mrs. Kelley says, picking up the paper and unfolding it across the table. "Let's see who died today," she says, turning to the obituaries on the next-to-last page. "Anybody we know?" she says.

This is an old worn out joke between them. If Mr. Kelley were his old self he would say "*I'm* not there. That's all I care." But instead he ignores her—for the second time today. (And he *didn't* forget that ice cube.) He slams the handle down on the electric can opener so it grinds its teeth all at once into the can.

The Billboard

MR. CUTTS knows if he tells Dolores over the phone that her mother is having an affair with the Marlboro Man, Dolores won't come. So he leaves the Marlboro Man out. He just tells her her mother is having an affair.

"An affair!"

"An affair."

"An *affair!* Dad, I don't believe you."

"Dolores, your mother is having an affair. I've seen them."

"Who have you seen; what have you seen them do?"

"Well—"

"Never mind, just let me speak to her."

"She's not here."

"Where is she?"

"Home."

"Home? Where are you?"

"In a phone booth, but don't worry. I only left her for a minute. She's taking a nap. If she woke up she might've listened on the extension. But Dolores," he went on, "I want you to know I've been keeping an eye on the whole sordid thing. I could have walked out on her, but I didn't. I only left her now because she was asleep. For an entire week she hasn't been two minutes out of my sight."

Dolores knows her mother isn't having an affair. Ever since she married and moved away eight years ago her father has been trying desperately to get her home. The first time he called he had cancer. "Cancer of the colon," he said, "my stools are red."

"Jesus Christ. Have you gone to see a doctor?"

"I don't need to see a doctor. My appetite is down. My temperature is up. Those are the signs, you know."

She left instructions with Larry how to mix formula for Jason and rode the bus up to New Hampshire. They broke the cancer news to her startled mother, and they all had a good cry. And then Dolores, woken by a noise early the next morning, got up and found him sitting at the kitchen table polishing off a whole serving bowl full of beets. So much for cancer of the colon.

This time Dolores knows what her father is up to, and yet there's nothing she can do but give in.

"All right, Dad, all right. Two days. No longer, do you hear? Larry's got an important business deal coming up in Columbus on Thursday and I won't take the kids out of school. I'll come home for two days, but that's it, understood?"

"Dolores, do you think I enjoy this? Do you think I enjoy being treated like a little kid?"

"Dad, look—" But as usual, there's nothing to say. "I'll be home on the bus tomorrow morning."

~

The Cuttses live in a split level ranch, the last house on Walker-Bungalow Road. Their backyard abuts the new interstate highway. This explains the billboard that overlooks their property.

As soon as Mr. Cutts hangs up, he fumbles for another dime and places a second call.

"So, what can be done?" he asks Walter.

"Well, is it already up?"

"Yes, it's already up! They put it up last weekend, I told you, now that the interstate is open."

"If it's already up, George, then it could be difficult. Too bad you and the others didn't petition," Walter says. Walter is Mr. Cutts' brother-in-law, a lawyer. "Then there would've been a complaint registered. That makes it easier later on, but I tell you what, George, I'll look into it. Is it obscuring your property in any way? I mean for instance does your television set still come in?"

"Louisa's garden doesn't get the sun in the afternoon any more. She's been talking about that already."

"That might work. I'll get back to you, okay, George? Just hold on."

~

At the dinner table when Dolores breaks the news, Larry calls her father a kook. Says she's crazy if she goes. He even turns on the kids: Jason, who is seven now, and Sarah, who is six. "Your grandfather is a *kook,*" he says, "and if your mother gives in to him he's going to keep on calling us, pulling these little stunts of his until he drives us all nuts!"

Both kids stop chewing and laugh.

"Don't you laugh," Dolores says. "For chrissake, Larry, it's their grandfather you're talking to them about."

"Dolores, just call the house and speak to your mother. You want me to call, I'll call, what's the number?"

"No. It would only upset her. I'm going," Dolores says, setting the milk pitcher on the table so the milk snaps up at her. "I told you, don't worry about your stupid business meeting in Columbus. I'll be home by Wednesday night. I'm going and that's it, so let's drop it," she says, into her glass. "I don't want to hear another word about it."

~

When the bus pulls onto Congress Street downtown, Dolores spots her father standing in front of the drugstore right away. He insists on carrying her bag. He takes her by the arm and leads her across the street into Moulton's, the old high school hangout Dolores hasn't been to in years. Everything looks exactly the same. Right down to Mr. Moulton behind the counter in his paper hat.

Once they're settled safely into a booth in the back, before Dolores can reach for a menu to see if they still have mocha frappes, her father shucks his coat and grabs her arm. He tells her to listen carefully, he has to hurry. Her mother is at the hairdresser's getting her hair done but is due back to meet him at any time. Then he begins to explain to her as rapidly as he can all of the fantastic things that have been going on.

"Dad, do you realize what you're saying?"

"I know it sounds crazy, but I *saw* it. One night after supper I was sitting in the den reading the paper when I heard these puckering sounds. When I went out into the kitchen your mother was squirming all over in front of the sink. Running her hands up and down her sides. Fiddling with her apron. Puckering and unpuckering her lips, like a goldfish. I snuck up behind her and looked out the window and there he was, looming out over the yard. His cigarette was hanging out of the corner of his mouth, he was still threading that lasso through his hands—but, Dolores, he was *winking* at your mother! He'd pushed his cowboy hat onto the back of his head. He was winking at her and he was clucking his tongue!"

Here Mr. Cutts sits back, letting go of Dolores' arm. He looks around to make sure no one is listening, and then, having caught his breath, he continues on.

"When your mother finally saw me she spun around and said hello. Hel*lo*, I said, but she didn't say anything else. So I pretended I hadn't seen a thing. I just asked her if she knew where the sports section was, though I had it all the time with the rest of the paper behind my back, and then I lay awake in bed all that night. Now I know what you're thinking, Dolores. At first I couldn't believe it either, but I *saw* it. I saw it! I said to myself. I decided that the next day at work I'd come down with the flu and head home early. I didn't pull up in the driveway, I parked at the curb, and when I came in the house was empty. I checked every single room just hoping it wasn't so, and then finally went into the kitchen and looked out the window. She was in the garden gardening, on her knees. With her gardening gloves on, with a spade in her hand and everything. Everything like always, *except*—except he'd shifted the loops of his lasso to one hand, he was reaching down and massaging her back with his finger! She was fluttering her eyes. I'm serious, Dolores, don't laugh!"

Dolores doesn't know what to make of it until it comes to her her father is pulling her leg. Until she remembers all of a sudden how when she was a kid he used to sit on her nightstand and tell her some of the weirdest bedtime stories she'd ever heard. Stories easily as weird as this.

"Boy, Dad, you're weird," she says. "You do *realize* what you're saying?"

"Of course I *realize* what I'm saying, but it's true! I called up your uncle yesterday after I talked to you, to see if he can get an injunction against the advertising agency or something, so they'll take it down, but he doesn't know. He thinks it may be too late. I didn't tell *him* why I want it gotten rid of, but I did think, Dolores, you'd believe me."

Just then the door jingles up front and her mother, her hair done, walks in.

Every time Dolores sees her she looks better. She was a plain woman while Dolores was growing up, but it's clear to Dolores, as to everyone else, that Louisa Cutts wears middle age well. With her hair done softly around her face, she looks like she might even have lost some weight.

Mr. Cutts slides over to make room for her in the booth, and then the two of them—Dolores (who is composing herself) and her father—do the best they can to convince her that Dolores just decided on a lark to come home. For a little visit. Larry is handling the kids. She needed a break, and anyway, how long has it been since the last time she visited—about a year? Dolores was going to call a cab to surprise them at the house, but she spotted her father walking around the Soldier's Park when the bus pulled in.

"...So, surprise!" Dolores says, after they've put together all the pieces of their shaky story.

"Well, it is a surprise," Mrs. Cutts says, folding her hands on her purse. "How long can you stay?"

"Oh, just a few days."

"Your father," Mrs. Cutts says "—did he tell you?—he's got a sore throat. He shouldn't even be out of the house, but he insisted on driving me into town. He promised he wouldn't walk around, that he'd go to the library and read the magazines and then come right here at eleven to meet me. But he was in the Soldier's Park, was he? Geo*rrr*ge."

Mr. Cutts doesn't try to defend himself.

"So how is Larry, anyway? How's Jason, and Sarah?" Mrs. Cutts, looking back at Dolores, suddenly says.

"Oh, they're fine. Well, Larry and I had a falling-out, but they're fine. Nothing serious," Dolores says. "Larry and I, I mean."

"I hope not," Mrs. Cutts says. Then leaning forward, "Did your father tell you that the new interstate has opened? We've got a billboard right out over the backyard!"

"Yes, he did," Dolores says as nonchalantly as possible. But she has to chew the side of her hand as if it itches, to keep from smiling.

"Well, I can't believe you're actually here! On a hunch I took a roast out of the freezer yesterday. I said to myself, why don't you take that roast out of the freezer? There was something in the air I guess. I knew that something was going to happen!"

Because the asphalt is still riddled with potholes from last winter, when Mr. Cutts pulls into Walker-Bungalow Road he has to slow the car way down. Dolores is riding in the back. Mrs. Cutts, up front on the passenger's side, turns around and faces her to speak.

"*There* it is," she says, whenever the thick beard of trees running alongside thins so that they can make out the cars flashing by. "See *there. There*," she says whenever a glimpse of the new highway whips past. "It shoots right up into Maine," she says, holding the back of the seat for support as Mr. Cutts pulls sharply up into their driveway. "If your father and I want to go to Boothbay," she says, turning to let herself out, "it shouldn't take us any more than two hours. Remember how miserable that old road was?"

"Doesn't the noise bother you?" Dolores asks. "All the trucks?"

"Not at all. And there's our billboard," she says. "See?"

It stands just over the north edge of their property anchored by a lattice of metal struts. It's difficult for Dolores to look at it without laughing. At the cowboy's jauntily cocked head. The crinkles at the corners of his giant eyes. The spanking white of his perfectly shaped teeth—

"But come on inside," Mrs. Cutts says, "first I want to show you the ceramics I've been working on. I've been going to a ceramic class on Friday nights."

In the kitchen when Mrs. Cutts has left the room, Mr. Cutts turns to Dolores and says, "Good, now that you're here I can take a shower. I haven't taken a shower all week."

When Mrs. Cutts has shown Dolores her ceramics, all sorts of little doodads she has made—"I didn't go last Friday because your father was sick, but usually I go every week"—she takes Dolores out into the back yard. She takes her heels off and leaves them on the mat on the back step and leads the way in stocking-feet to her garden. "Oh, I'm having a great time with it," she says, crouching to examine a row of tiny cukes on one side. "It's the first time I've enjoyed the upkeep—all the weeding!—in years."

At the bottom edge of the property, Dolores notices, there's a red, wooden slatted fence a little worse for wear. On the other side of that is the highway, quite a change from when Dolores was growing up. "Wow," Dolores says. "I wonder what they did with that old tree trunk I used to play in?"

"Oh they're going to replace *that* ugly thing." Getting up, Mrs. Cutts didn't hear what she said, she only saw where Dolores was looking. "Any day now." She's brushing her hands together, smoothing her stockings. "With a chain-link. I'm like a little kid again. I can't wait."

If her mother is getting along better than ever over the years, Dolores is becoming even less sure about her father. At the dinner table she keeps studying him over her plate. She wonders if it's all in her imagination, or do his glasses really look too big? Since she saw him last haven't his cheeks sunk in, just a little? Oh, how can I blame him? she thinks. How can anyone blame him? He only does it because he misses me so much he wants to see me back!

After dinner, Mr. Cutts goes into the den with the paper, and Dolores and her mother do the dishes. This is Dolores' big chance to speak up, but she's decided not to, she's decided to keep quiet. I'll stay till tomorrow, just relax and enjoy myself, she thinks, and well, if that will make him happy, what could be wrong with that?

"See, and that's what it looks like when it's all lit up! Isn't it something?" Mrs. Cutts says, letting her hands go still in the soapy water. "Who would've thought even two years ago when all you could see out this window was trees that there'd ever be a highway full of cars! And a billboard right out over the back yard twice as big as a movie screen!"

Dolores smiles at her mother. She leans over the dishboard and looks with her out the window. There's a white string of headlights stretching along the highway. A row of floodlights shining on the wide advertisement that seem for a minute to add a glint to the cowboy's blue eyes.

"Quite a sight, isn't it?" her mother says.

Dolores nods. "Yes," she says. She takes a handful of silver out of her mother's hand and dries each piece individually with the towel. It's good to be home. Good to be home, and besides, Dolores thinks, dropping the dried silver noisily into the drawer and boosting it shut, it'll do Larry some good for a change to have a taste of taking care of his kids.

~

When Dolores and her mother go into the den, Mr. Cutts is sitting on the footstool adjusting the television. Phil Silvers is one of the guests on Merv Griffin. As Mr. Cutts, finally satisfied with the color, is settling back into his chair, Merv reaches over and wiggles his finger through Phil's glasses. "*Phil*," he says, "what *happened* to your glasses?"

"I don't need glasses. I don't wear glasses. Just frames."

"*Why?*" Merv says.

"Because otherwise no one would know who I am, *dummy*."

He takes them off and looks for the camera. Sure enough. To Dolores he looks like Mr. McNabb. Mr. McNabb owns the butcher shop downtown.

Mr. Cutts gets a kick out of this. "He does," he says.

And later when the show is over, when Mr. Cutts is flipping the channels for something else for them to watch, he says, "So Phil Silvers doesn't need glasses. Imagine that, wearing glasses for nothing. Huh!"

It's after this that Dolores remembers Larry. She thought she had better call him when she finished the dishes, but forgot.

"Who'd your father think the sucker was, anyway?"

When Larry says this, she hangs up.

~

Around eleven, when all three of them are weak from laughter from listening to Mr. Cutts retell about the time he got stuck in Smiley's Market when an old man ran in gone berserk with a hatchet (so he had to duck down behind the bread rack and hide), they turn out the downstairs lights and head up the stairs to bed.

At the landing Dolores kisses her parents goodnight—the first time she's kissed her parents goodnight in years—and then turns down the hall toward her room.

When she's changed into her nightgown and brushed her teeth, still chuckling occasionally from the hatchet story her father told (the man who went berserk accused poor Smiley of making moves on his ugly old wife), Dolores climbs up the ladder and gets into bed. She had bunk beds when she was a girl growing up and she'd always slept on the top.

Maybe I *won't* go home Wednesday, she thinks, nestling in. Maybe I'll just stay for a few days.

Amazed at how easy it would be—she could just call home in the morning, tell him something has come up, see how Mr. Wiseguy likes that—and reaches down and turns off the light on the nightstand where her father telling her his stories used to sit, and proceeds to drift just as easily toward sleep.

When Mr. and Mrs. Cutts have settled under their covers, Mr. Cutts reaches out and turns the lamp off between them.

Everything's going to be okay now, he thinks. Louisa believes Dolores came on her own, she doesn't realize that I suspect anything. And as soon as Walter gets the thing taken down everything will settle back to normal, for good. By God, if I have to, he thinks, I *will* go around to the neighbors with a petition.

Everything is going to be okay, he thinks. Everything—okay, he thinks, as he lies on his back facing the ceiling, the air gradually catching in his throat. First in hiccups, the furry segments, then he's snoring at a regular pace.

She waits a bit once he's started, and then quietly she slips out of bed. She wraps her housecoat around her and steps into her slippers lying in wait by the closet. She tiptoes down the stairs. Through the den. Through the kitchen and out the back door, freezing for a full minute on the back step when the screen accidentally slams shut behind her.

He's afraid to pick her up with his fingers. He takes the cigarette out of the corner of his mouth and gently holds it out towards her. It's huge. She walks up and reaches around it with both arms. She kicks her slippers off onto the lawn and hooks her feet over the filter.

He picks her way up into the air and puckers his lips and begins to blow on her. Until her eyes sparkle and tears run across her cheeks. He waves her around and around—up over the house, over the garden, out over the highway—as each of the cars one after another slow down and hit their lights. As one after another, amazed, they lumber awkwardly onto the shoulder.

As Dolores, wakened by the slammed door, decides she had better get up. As she tosses back her covers. Climbs carefully down out of bed. As Dolores, still thinking gaily to herself See how Mr. WiseGuy likes *that!*, feels her way across the dark room to lift the shade.

A Couple of Granite Staters Bump into One Another In a Bar in San Francisco

Pete

"I'm from New Hampshire," he tells the bartender, who is rinsing a tray of glasses in front of him.

All week long whenever he made this announcement, he was amused by the comments it brought. *New Hampshire. No kidding. Now, where is that exactly?* Or: *New Hampshire. New Hampshire? Oh, right. That's that little state that's shaped like a harp.*

He was amused that the place he came from seemed to others (for some reason) so exotic.

But not to the bartender. "Oh really?" he says. "Then you've got to meet Felicia. She's from the old Granite State, too."

"Excuse me?"

"Felicia," the bartender says. He's a pale, dark-haired fellow. He's wearing jeans and a sleeveless tee-shirt, and he has a ragged strip of black leather tied around one arm. He's busy drying his hands, so he uses his elbow to point down the bar to where a half-dozen bleary-eyed old men are gathered around a woman much younger—a handsome, leggy blonde in a hip-hugging silver lamé dress whose hair is done up so high in a flip on one side and who, while their eyes are on her, stops talking just long enough to take a drag on her cigarette, then, recommencing, blows smoke through her nose.

"Really?"

"*She* says," the bartender shrugs, just as the old men double over in an explosion of laughter and the blonde, her hair like a giant teapot, upon seeing she has their attention as well, raises her glass and tinkles her ice.

"So, Pete, you too? Howzabout another?"

"What? Well sure, Ron. It was Ron, wasn't it?" He's met so many people this week!

"That's moi," the bartender says.

"S*uu*re. I'll have another. I shouldn't really. I've got a little paperwork I've got to do back at the hotel before bed. And then I've got to pack. But hey, what the heck? I guess I'm entitled to a good time just as much as the next guy. Aren't I?"

He's been in town for the hobby convention at the Hyatt at Embarcadero two blocks away (he owns a place called *The Hobby Hut* back home, and with a little luck hopes to open up *The Hobby Hut Too* at a local mall that's soon to go in out on what used to be the old county fairgrounds not far from where he lives), but, as he tells Ron while Ron pours him his drink, today was the convention's last day. And so he has a plane he has to catch in the morning. This wasn't, however, the 'original' plan.

"*Originally* my wife was supposed to join me," he says. "We'd made all these arrangements to do the city up big and then rent a car and drive down the coast. Stop at Carmel, is it? Big Sur. San Simeon. San Simeon," he repeats, "I was looking forward to that. Friends who were out last summer told us to be sure not to miss it. But my wife, she just called me this morning to tell me she wouldn't be coming. One of the kids came down with the measles. What rotten luck, huh? I told her to just leave him with his grandmother as planned. But no. No way! she said. And so all our arrangements, the itinerary we'd worked on for months, everything finito, ka*put!*" He rolls his eyes and sips from his glass. "So, Ron, tell me," he says, "do you have any kids?"

The bartender chuckles. "No. No kids," he says.

"A wife?"

"No." (More chuckles.) "No wife."

"Good for you!" Pete says. But the bartender is off with the blonde woman's drink. And again her friends are howling like maniacs, apparently having one jolly old time.

~

It's only half-past nine, but to Pete it feels like it's later. This afternoon (after the argument with his wife) he accepted the invitation of a board-game salesman and, with a couple of other fellows, retailers from Long Island, went to dinner at a place near here called Metro. Formerly an automobile dealership, it had just recently been converted, their host had told them, into one of San Francisco's swankier restaurants.

But, in spite of its fancy surroundings, and the excellent posture of its white-gloved waiters, their meal there still managed to degenerate rather quickly into a string of dirty jokes. It left Pete with a funny taste in his mouth and the feeling that once again this city was testing him somehow. Challenging him to loosen his tie and roll up his sleeves and be as bad as he possibly dared.

Since he arrived last Monday morning (he can hardly believe it, but, as he sits here reviewing the particulars now, he realizes that yes, it's true), three women have thrown themselves at him, and all of them (the killer) were married! One was a saleswoman for a model airplane company, and the other two, whom he met while browsing the booths, managed hobby stores just like his. Pete didn't even recognize their advances at first, but, from what he gathered from that night's dinner conversation *not* aimed at a bawdy punchline, his dining companions did.

And well, so what? he thinks.

Then: But could such a fling—a one shot in a faraway

city with someone you'd never set eyes on again—could it really be very satisfying? he wonders. Recalling what happened later: Well, no, he thinks, apparently not.

There was an X-rated theater across the street showing a movie called *In Diana Jones*, and after their dessert had been served, his companions made a bee-line right for it.

Pete bowed out graciously, however, and walked himself back towards the hotel.

The downtown streets were deserted almost, but the city still wouldn't give up. Since he had resisted its urge that he cheat on his wife, it seemed determined to shock his sensibilities at least in whatever way it could.

Within a block, he passed a woman—a girl, really—with a mohawk the color of Pepto-Bismol and with arms covered with tattoos as bright as the Sunday funnies. And then, just after, he passed another. This girl, a little older perhaps, wore her hair cropped painfully short and was dressed, head-to-toe, in black. She had black circles painted raccoon-like around each of her eyes, and she wore large hoop earrings which were by far the largest hoop earrings Pete had ever seen. They were huge. They bumped heavily against her black-clad shoulders. Parrots could have swung in them, he thought.

But what was worse than any of this was that even the familiar Pete passed was often disarmingly odd.

A little further on (for example) he passed a distinguished looking, gray-haired businessman who was dressed in a suit and tie. Perfectly normal, of course, except that the man was carrying a purse—a dazzling sequinned number—from which he casually withdrew a set of car keys before ducking into an all-night garage.

And then Pete passed a barbershop that could have been anywhere. It had a barber pole outside. It had the ox-red leather chairs with the white metal piping. It had the deep-bellied porcelain sink with the swan-necked spigot set against the wall in the back. It had the calendar hung over the cash register that read "McKeown Plumbing—Call Us Anytime—24 Hrs. A Day." But, though its lights were blaring, it was empty inside (the sign on the door read CLOSED), save the barber, a middle-aged man in a pale blue smock with snaps, who was sitting in the center chair playing a clarinet. Not *playing*—Pete could have handled that. His song, or whatever you'd call it, was a *wail.* His eyes seemed ready to pop out. His cheeks were as red and as hard as apples. It was a tune that Pete couldn't have recognized if given a million years. It was a dipping, curving something.

Sitting at the bar, he shudders at the recollection even. The whole thing gives him the creeps.

It was just after that, as Pete neared his hotel, that at last he caught sight of something he thought he could probably trust. It was a tiny, unpretentious Tudor-styled building squeezed between the shoulders of two steep, glass-faced towers. Even its sign was comforting. Scrolled on wood, plain, nothing fancy, it read simply: YE OLDE PUB.

It was early—not to mention, he reminded himself, his last night. Packing would take ten minutes, max. And the few invoices he needed to fill out? Another twenty, at most. A half hour, Pete figured, wouldn't hurt. And he deserved it! Of that, he was sure.

Inside, it was dark, smoky, but sweet-smelling, too. Given it was Friday, it wasn't as crowded as Pete thought it might be, and the group there was curiously mixed. All of the women (of which there were only a handful) looked like they were dressed for the opera—as spectators *or* participants, it was hard to tell which—but the men, thankfully, were dressed less formally. In fact, there were a lot of loose-knit sweaters, and a slew of pleated pants. But there were also just enough dressed almost exactly like Pete (slacks, sportcoat, tie) to help him let his guard down. At last he felt nearly at home.

Felicia

"So, Ron tells me you're from New Hampshire," she says as she deposits her drink on the bar top and settles onto a stool right beside him.

"That's right," he answers, startled. He hadn't seen her approach.

"So, from where in New Hampshire? I'm from Baystown," she says.

"You're kidding." He just looks at her. "*I'm* from Baystown," he says. And thus immediately whatever she hoped might happen between them is drastically, irrevocably revised.

She's removing the cellophane from a fresh pack of cigarettes, but at the familiar sound of his voice, coupled with this unsettling news, she stops herself cold for a minute—and then wishes she were wearing her glasses. From a distance he certainly looked handsome enough, but up close, thanks to a case of farsightedness that's only gotten worse through the years, he's nothing but a life-sized blur.

"You *are* kidding me, aren't you?" he asks.

"No. I don't think so," she says, meaning perhaps she should pretend that she is.

When he tells her his name (excitedly), that clinches it. Unbelievable! she thinks, it's him. The same guy she pined for from afar all through high school—what? twenty? *nearly* twenty years ago! But still, there's no need to panic, she tells herself. No. At least not yet.

"How do you do?" she says, evenly. "My name is—Felicia Andrews."

"Andrews?" he says. "You're joking!"

She crosses her legs and taps a cigarette from the pack in her hands. He couldn't really remember her, could he? Ha. *Hardly*, she thinks. "No," she says, preparing her lighter, "I'm not."

"Andrews? *Andrews?* Really?"

"Yes," she says. Then she can't help herself: "*Really!*"

"Then I know you!" He can barely sit still. "You lived on Wentworth Road. I can't believe it! Wow! *I know you!*"

Uh-oh, she thinks, but smiles. "You do, do you?" she says.

"Yes! Yes, I do! I went to school with your brother. Felix. I didn't know him that well," he says, "but I did. We were in the same class at Baystown High. Felix Andrews. You're his sister—right?"

Having lit her cigarette, she turns away from her old heart-throb for a minute and releases one long plume of smoke.

"You are, aren't you?" he says.

Christ, she thinks. Why me?

"Of course you are! You look just like him," he says. "I knew that Felix had a sister," he says, "but I thought her name was Elizabeth—Marybeth—*Something*-beth. Anyway, Felice, you said?"

"Felicia," she corrects him, huskily.

"Felicia! I can't believe it," he says, leaning back. Looking at her, but not recognizing her apparently. He says, "The chances—do you know what the *chances* must be of bumping into someone you know in a big-time city like this?"

Exactly. The chances! she thinks.

And then they both just sit there, dazed. Partly thinking, yes, about the odds of such a meeting, and partly not sure, either of them, what in the world they might possibly say next.

Her situation is the more delicate, however; she wishes to God she had never walked over. For one thing, it was her friends who dared her into this predicament, and her friends (whose eyes haven't left her since she got up to make her move) who will very likely razz her to death if they find out who he is.

What luck! she thinks, fiddling with the ice in her glass, when suddenly he says, "So, Felix—"

Ah, well, that's it. It's taken him long enough, she thinks. But, no.

"*Felix Andrews*," he says. "There's a name I haven't said out loud in a while! How is old Felix, anyway. He left town right after high school. Went into the Marines or something, right?"

"Oh, Felix?" she says. She takes a drink. "Felix. Well, Felix is—gone."

"Oh? *Oh.* I'm sorry."

"No. It's okay," she says. "It's not what you think. He's not—"

Then: Well, she might as well just leave it. *Hell,* she thinks, why not? She waves one ringed hand back towards the blackened window behind them, and it's then, within the space of that simple gesture, that Felicia realizes not one thing, but two: first, that if he hasn't recognized her (thank God!), he *has* remembered her; and second, that this, if she'd had a little time to think about it, is exactly how she would have hoped it would be.

"So, *Pete*," she says—she's really touched, he remembered her!—"what did you say you're doing in California?"

"I didn't," he says, "I don't think!"

And after he told her about the hobby convention and his store and the branch he plans to open, and about his kids and his house and his wife, he says, "Say, I bet you know her. Nancy Sherman was her maiden name. She grew up in Baystown, too!"

The threat of her friends which has receded quite a bit already recedes completely now—now that it's her turn to get all excited.

"Nancy Sherman. You're kidding! Of course!"

"You were friends?"

"Sort of," she says. "I mean, Nancy and Felix were, sort of," she says, figuring she better back-pedal some. "They were lab partners in biology one year. *The Year of the Frog*," she announces.

"Oh, really?" he says.

But she doesn't answer. She just laughs a little thinking

about it, both she and Nancy scared still by the thing, the white throat and the fist-sized belly, pinned flat to their dissecting pan.

After a bit, though, she shudders this part of the recollection aside and, lifting her cigarette, smiling, she says, "She was nice. Friendly. Nancy."

"Yes. Well, maybe," he says, "but to tell you the truth I'm a little mad at her right now."

She raises her eyebrows.

"She finked out on me," he says, and then he tells her about their plans, all ditched at the very last minute. "But anyway," he says when he's finished, "enough about us—me. What is it *you*'re doing in California?"

"Well. I live here," she says. And then, after she's told him where (a neighborhood he has never heard of), "I work for the telephone company."

"No fooling. An operator?" he asks.

"Not exactly. I drive a truck."

He laughs. "That's funny," he says. "No wonder you're such a hit with your friends."

"But I do!" she says, flicking an ash into the ash tray. She straightens her shoulders so that her dress sparkles gently all over. Then, adjusting the clutter of her bracelets, "I'm a pole climber," she tells him proudly.

"Really?"

"Really."

He shakes his head.

"What? You don't believe me?"

"Oh, I believe you," he says, "but a good-looking woman like you climbing up a telephone pole!" He shakes his head some more. "I take it you dress a bit differently for work?"

"Quite differently," she says. "You're right about that."

"Well, it's been a heck of a week, let me tell you!" And then he tells her just for instance about the spooky, clarinet-playing barber.

"Oh yes, of course. I know him."

"You do?"

"Yes. Around here he's a celebrity," she says. "He's a regular old barber by day—and presto! Benny Goodman by night. All power to him." She raises her drink. "That's what we say, anyway. Don't you?"

But before he can answer another woman has come up behind them, this one an Ann Miller look-alike whom Pete noticed standing by the jukebox when he first walked into the place. She has a blue-black bouffant, and she's wearing a bright red blazer and black stretch pants with elastic stirrups. Plus dangerous, six-inch heels.

"Excuse me, honey," she says (this to Felicia, though looking sideways at Pete), "but before I split I thought I should check. We're still on for tomorrow, right? The Veteran's Day Clearance at Sak's?"

"Yes, Dusty," Felicia says patiently.

"Just thought I'd check," she says, then stands there.

Until Felicia says, obligingly, "Dusty, this is Pete. Pete, as I'm sure you know by now, this here is Dusty."

"Hi, sugar," Dusty says. "You know, you can come too if you want. All their evening wear—slashed to half price!"

"Thanks," Pete says, "but—"

"*Bye*, Dusty," Felicia says. And after Dusty has left: "By day, Dusty is a stockbroker. Very successful. Believe it or not!"

Pete doesn't believe it, but Felicia nods, and, draining her drink, signals to Ron for another. "And Ron-Bon," she calls down the bar, "hit Pete again, too. It looks like he needs it. My treat."

Of the two drinks soon delivered, Felicia's is the tall, aqua-colored concoction, a paper parasol stuck jauntily in its top. It's certainly not your basic pub sort of drink, but Pete, finally relaxed in this big strange city, doesn't seem to notice. He says, "Hey Ron, how about this? I knew Felicia's brother. We went to school together. Felix Andrews!"

Ron, surprised, rests one elbow on the bar. "You knew Felicia *already*?"

"Not Felicia," Pete clarifies, "her brother."

But when the both of them look at her for some corroboration—well, didn't he just call her good-looking? Ordinarily, Felicia would have been hopelessly smitten, but under the circumstances (what *are* the chances of something like this ever happening? she wonders), she's merely hopeless, giddy. She takes another deep-throated drag on her cigarette, and then just looks back at them both and smiles.

"Oh, right. You knew *Felix*," Ron says, and pushes himself back up. He nods and then a laugh breaks out. He catches it, though, and diligently mops up around them. When he heads back toward Felicia's friends, however, he can't hold it in any longer. By the time he has joined the huddle that anxiously awaits his report, his shoulders are shaking already.

To Felicia who's dreamily stirring her drink: "I didn't think it was that funny," Pete says, "but it certainly *is* amazing."

And yes, of course, it is!

For the next hour, hour and a half almost, the two of them don't even notice the hoots that rip from Felicia's friends.

Pete couldn't be happier to talk about home—of course he's been missing it like crazy all week, regardless of his recent argument with Nancy.

And Felicia—well, Felicia is genuinely surprised at all she remembers (and fondly!) about a place which when she left it eighteen years ago she vowed to forget.

Bartlett's Ice Cream Stand is gone, and the municipal pool on Pierce Island is full up with weeds, but there are still Moe's Italian sandwiches and Mrs. Larrabee's Raspberry Pies.

Lafayette Road—you wouldn't recognize *it*, she's told, but downtown Baystown hasn't changed that much. George & Phillip's. The Victory Spa. Green's Pharmacy. Tessa's Fabulous Dresses. Yes, they're all still there.

What about Greyhound? Greyhound has gone. But not Trailways, Pete points out. At least not Trailways *yet.*

It's the same with the names that pop up.

Ricky Simpson. Becky Quayle. Ed Reese.

Tom Parks. Gary Engle. Danielle Splaine.

A few have left, but more, by far, have stayed, most having coupled in combinations which, when you stop and think, Felicia realizes, were as predictable as Nancy and Pete.

In fact, when you get right down to it, and as pleasant as it is to reminisce in this way, Felicia realizes that nothing Pete has said is actually too surprising. Eighteen years could have just as likely been eighteen minutes for all that's changed in Baystown since she rode the bus into Concord that long-ago Monday and signed up with the U.S. Marines.

In just a little more than an hour, she's all caught up so that the ruckus her friends are still making, though not as wild and uproarious as earlier, manages to capture their attention once more and pull the both of them back down to earth.

"Gosh, will you look at the time," Pete says (though it's early, only five till eleven). "And I promised myself a half hour." Then, glancing up the bar to where the old men are in the middle of a real snorter, "They have certainly been enjoying themselves!"

"What's that? Oh, them," Felicia says. "To them, everything is hilarious." She toasts her friends with her drink as she says this, and all of them, watery-eyed, winking, toast back. "But after a while it can get kind of boring," she says. "Ron-Bon!" she calls, raising her glass yet again. Then to Pete: "Are you sure you don't want just one more?"

"Thanks, but no, I can't," Pete says. "The only flight I was able to book back home leaves at 8:15."

Pete took his jacket off a while ago and laid it across the empty barstool beside him, but as he's reaching for it now he stops. There is something else he has been meaning to say, but hasn't had a chance.

"Your brother—"

"My brother?"

"Yes, your brother," Pete says. "I really am awfully sorry. He certainly was a character, you know."

Felicia isn't at all sure she wants to hear this (*a character?*), but suddenly Pete is laughing.

"What, what is it?" she asks.

It's a minute, though, before Pete can pull himself together enough to speak.

"Sorry," he says finally, wiping his eyes, "but I just remembered the time he came to high school in bell-bottoms. He was the first one in Baystown to wear them, remember? When was that? 1967? Bell-bottoms! Remember bell-bottoms?" he cries. "Gosh, they were strange looking things!" He laughs a little more. "The first *and* the last, I think," he says. And then, getting a grip on himself, "But, you know, Felice—"

"Felicia," she corrects him, tersely.

"Felicia," he repeats, "I'm sorry. But you know, that wasn't what I was going to say. There's something else about your brother that I *hadn't* forgotten. Something I don't think I've ever told anyone—no, I'm sure I haven't—ever before."

"Oh?" she says, warily, "what's that?"

And what he tells her she hasn't forgotten either, though of course she doesn't say.

"Well, it's a stupid story," he starts in, "but once in high school I was accused of cheating. And I did cheat, I'm afraid. I sat behind your brother in Chem 101, and during an exam I wasn't prepared for I copied all of his answers. Felix didn't know anything about it of course, but when the teacher, Miss Griswold, called us up after class the next day and hit us with some pretty hard evidence—we had all the same answers correct and all the same answers wrong—well, *I* was ready to confess and beg forgiveness, but Felix spoke up first.

"He told her that we had studied together, and that that explained the identical scores. This though we weren't even friends! Had hardly ever spoken even! She was skeptical at first of course—who wouldn't be?—but then he asked her if he could see his exam. And when she'd given it to him he turned to me and he said, 'What did I tell you? Sulfur dioxide *is* liquefiable! But you *insisted* your notes said it wasn't.'" Pete laughs. "Or something like that," he says, "and I said, 'Oh. Yeah. Sorry.' Then we went over the other answers in the same way for a bit, and ha! the Griz—she bought it! Heck, *I* bought it for a minute," he says. "He sounded so sincere. We were as chummy as chummy can be. *Until* Miss Griswold gave us both a B+ and then apologized to each of us for 'doubting our word,' as she put it, and said that we could go.

"You see, Felicia," he says, making sure he gets her name right this time. "You see, that's as long as we were friends, I'm afraid. I don't think I even thanked him. To tell you the truth, I know I didn't. I meant to, I think—I hope—but as soon as we were out in the hall I bolted down the stairwell—chemistry was last period, and I was late for baseball practice—and then later I just continued to treat Felix the same way everyone else treated Felix. Except for Nancy, I guess. You know," he says, tracing the rim of his glass, "I really never knew they were friends!"

Well, friends *sort of*, she wants to correct him, since that relationship too was more than likely as one-sided. But she's so struck that he's remembered any of this after all these years, that before she can say anything he's already moved on.

"I just ignored him. Or else I laughed along with everybody else at his crazy clothes. Not only the bell-bottoms, but the Nehru jackets. Remember Nehru jackets? And the turtleneck dickies. God! Remember them? With wooden beads no less. And those hideous plastic pendants!" Pete, made incredulous by the recollection, can only shake his head. "Can you i*ma*gine anyone ever dressing like that?"

There's a bit of silence all around them. Even Felicia's friends are watching quietly for a change, sobered by the icy look that has settled on Felicia's face.

But Pete saves himself, just in time. "Still, he was a good egg really," he says. He slides his glass away and reaches for his coat. "That's all I wanted to say. A little *weird*, if you don't mind my saying so. Really! Do you *remember* his get-ups?" He laughs a little more, then shimmies his arms into the sleeves of his jacket. "But I've never forgotten that he saved my neck. And, honestly, I've always felt bad that I never had the guts to thank him. Anyway—Viet Nam, was it?"

Felicia is puzzled at this at first, then nods. Here was the Baystown she had managed not to think of for years, and she regrets he has brought it all up.

"Well, I'm awfully sorry to hear that," Pete says, "*but*, on a jollier note, just wait till I tell Nancy who I bumped into! She won't believe it either! You look good by the way," he says, "did I say that? That dress, and your hair—it really is something. It's—well, amazing!"

She smiles and can't help but admire it herself in the mirror hung the length of the bar.

"Well, I had better be off," Pete says. Standing up, digging out his wallet, he has a little trouble getting Ron's attention. "Thanks, buddy," he says. "How much do I owe you?"

Then to Felicia, who's stamping out her cigarette, he says, "Well, I sure am glad I bumped into you. Frankly, I was beginning to worry about this town. Friends of ours love it," he says, "but I don't know, I just wasn't sure. Anyway," he says, "my faith is restored."

Felicia laughs, uneasily. "Yes, well, listen," she says, clearing her throat, her voice returned to her at last, "if you won't let me buy you another drink, at least you'll let me walk you to the door."

There's a gasp and elbow-jabbing among Felicia's friends when the both of them are standing together, but Felicia couldn't really care less. At the door when Pete shakes her hand, her bracelets jingle and her hair—it truly is amazing—a soft, shiny helmet as pale as the winter sun—blinks blue in the flashing light of a Chinese Take-Out sign across the street.

"So, take care!" Pete says.

But Felicia follows him outside (first out of the view of

her friends, and then out of earshot of their whistles and cackling) and, grabbing hold of both of his shoulders, plants one good smack on his cheek.

"Ha!" Pete says, flustered. Then, though they both know his heart isn't in it: "Listen, it's still pretty early. Have you ever been in the hotel where I'm staying? It's amazing. There's a waterfall, a whole lagoon really, in the bar. How about *I* buy *you* a drink?"

"Oh, that's sweet," she says, "but I can't. You see—it's my birthday!" she says. "And my friends—"

"No problem!" he says. Then: "It's your birthday? Really? Well, happy birthday!"

Fidgeting with an earring: "Oh, sure. I mean yes. Well, thanks."

"So—take care!" he says again, heading off.

"You, too," she says, watching him go. "And say hello to New Hampshire for me! Granite-Staters are rare birds around here, you know!"

Turning around so that now she can see that yes, it is him, he lifts his hand to wave. "You're right there!" he calls back to her, laughing. "*Ha!* Tell me about it!"

Pete

As soon as he rounds the corner, his hotel looms overhead like the prow of some brightly lit ship. Most would be thrilled to be in this city, to be staying in this fancy hotel, but Pete is looking forward to being home already. For one thing, Nancy—it's true. He never knew she and Felix Andrews were friends! At least Nancy had the guts not to shun him, he thinks. And for another—well, that kiss. Not to mention what he almost let happen. He takes out his handkerchief and wipes the lipstick from his face. That darn kiss, this darn city, he's thinking, when it hits him.

*Anna*beth. *Annabeth Andrews.* Wasn't that it? Felix's sister? Yes, yes it was.

And, come to think of it, it's Annabeth still. She's one of the tellers at Baystown Savings. A quiet, plain woman. Nondescript—no wonder she so slipped his mind. Wears glasses. A rather mousy brunette.

Felicia

After he's gone, she stands outside for a minute to gather her wits. There was as much spite in that kiss as gratitude, she realizes. But hey, look what it could've gotten her, if she had wanted it to.

It certainly has been a memorable evening, a once-in-a-lifetime evening! It's not her birthday, of course, but it should be. May everyone have an evening just like it, just once, she is thinking when, at the risk of spoiling it all, she straightens her stockings and heads back inside. She retrieves her cigarettes and what's left of her drink from where she and Pete were sitting, and then she swaggers back to her cronies.

"Not a word," she says as she hops up onto her barstool amongst them. "One fucking word and I'm out of here. I mean it."